ZAT

Killer Instinct

—◆—

Ben Zhen

For book orders, email orders@traffordpublishing.com.sg

Most Trafford Singapore titles are also available at major online book retailers.

Printed in Singapore.

ISBN: 978-1-4907-0238-4 (sc)
ISBN: 978-1-4907-0239-1 (hc)
ISBN: 978-1-4907-0240-7 (e)

Trafford rev. 12/02/2013

Tr**ffₓ**fford   www.traffordpublishing.com.sg

Singapore
toll-free: 800 101 2656 (Singapore)
Fax: 800 101 2656 (Singapore)

Contents

Foreword

The world is subjected to very subtle deceptions. Even as I start to write this fourth book, the 'Global Elite' is working behind the scenes, to bring about Satan's empire on earth. The 'Global Elite' knows full well that the world at large is oblivious to what is really happening, until it is too late.

This book is inspired by actual events that will bring in the New World Order. Nevertheless, it is largely a work of fiction. Some of the materials in this book came from research done during the writing of my earlier books.

We now live in a deceptive world which is ultimately ruled by Satan. Britain's Satanic Prime Minister, Sir Winston Churchill, had the vantage of our world of deception when he said that sometimes the truth is so precious, it must be attended by a bodyguard of lies. This is the principle of secret societies that only the elite (i.e. those initiated into the higher ranks) are privileged to know the secret truths. Clearly, Satan's character is opposite to that of Jesus Christ who is the light of the world. Jesus wants to disclose all truth to everyone so that all men are set free. "And You will know the truth, and the truth will set you free." **(John 8:32)**

Present day Israel was established by the followers of the Babylonian Talmud religion which is the basis of modern witchcraft. It would be only a matter of time when a Luciferian One World Government is established. Unknown to many people on earth, there are already political leaders who are followers of Satan; and they are complicit with secret Luciferian societies to impose a New World (Satanic) Order.

Introduction

This is the first thriller book that I have ever written. The inspiration to write this book is triggered by real events. In fact, actual names of persons has been used to give the story an appearance of reality. The fictional story of this book pales in comparison to the fabricated accounts dished out by the media, concerning the events of this world. In particular, the deceptions described by Jesus Christ as the "yeast of the Scribes and the Pharisees" is key to understanding much of the events that has unfolded recently.

Since I wrote my first book, much more Satanic deceptions came to light. It is extremely difficult to fathom Satan's actual agenda for this period. However, the final goal of Satan is to bring about the New World Order. Since the big lie of Satan in the garden of Eden, there is warfare between the forces of God and the forces of Satan. Hence, Satan had woven layers of lies to conceal his every planned action.

Fictional characters and fabricated events are included to protect the guilty. Any resemblance to actual persons and happenings are pure coincidences.

I decided to adopt the title of this book as "ZAT Killer Instinct" where ZAT is an abbreviation for 'Z Assassination Team.' The major force behind the historical events of the previous century, is the organization of international "banksters" (bankers who are gangsters). Through false flag operations and the strategy of chaos, these banksters have infiltrated into major countries and global institutions. The wars of this modern world is fought both in the physical space as well as cyberspace. For the first time in history, we see acts of terrorism committed by virtual groups. Hence, the concept of the 'Trojan Horse' is applicable both to the physical world and the virtual world. Since 1967, the banksters started to establish counterfeit Jerusalem.

In accordance to His timing God will destroy counterfeit Jerusalem which is figuratively described as Egypt and Sodom. This was revealed to John who was the apostle of Jesus Christ. This revelation is now available to all mankind in the book of Revelation which is the last chapter of the bible. "The revelation of Jesus Christ, which God gave him to show his servants what must soon take place. Jesus Christ made it known by sending his angel to his servant John, who testifies to everything he witnessed in accordance to the word of God and the testimony of Jesus Christ. Those who read the words of this prophecy and even those who hear the words of this prophecy shall be blessed, if they take to heart this prophecy, because the time is near." **(Rev. 1:1–3)**

1

Bolshevik Revolution Phase 2

After World War 2, the Nazi Phoenix rose from the ashes of Hitler's war machine called IG Farben and their industrial espionage unit called NW7. This was due to the work of UK's Victor Rothschild who got Prince Bernhard of the Netherlands to set up the Bilderberg Group which was a rich Royalist's Club in Europe and the largest Corporation owners networking society in the world. As a result, there was a rebirth of NW7 as PERMINDEX or Permanent Industrial Expositions. In the US, a similar group known as the "8F" group was established. The 8F group had notable members like Bobby Baker, Billy Sol Estes, Robert Kerr, Clint Merchinson, HL Hunt, George Smathers, Lawrence Bell, Richard Russell, George Brown, Herman Brown, **Lyndon B. Johnson**, **John Connally**, Fred Korth and many extreme right wing political players that helped to fix various US Government contracts like Naval Fuel supply contracts and jet fighters.

During the time of F. D. Roosevelt, the OSS was controlled by his son Kermit Roosevelt and Bill Donovan who were American patriots. The CIA was formed from the downsizing of the British dominated OSS. After F. D. Roosevelt's death, British elements and the Zionists recruited Truman who took over the US Presidency. Truman filled the CIA with Wall Street and British Spooks, with the help of J. Edgar Hoover. Hence, the CIA ended up with a faction of American Patriots like Donovan, Colby, Casey versus James Angleton, Helms, Dulles who were all British aligned agents and part of the Truman Wall Street crowd. Truman set off a political shift in America that was more about British and Zionist Foreign Interests than US interest. As the 8F group was related to PERMINDEX, it was supported by the Anglo-Zionist faction of the CIA.

PERMINDEX as the European Royalist's principle Intelligence group caused the ouster of Batista and ushered in Castro who was initially popular in the US. In 1960, Castro imported a million barrels of Russian oil to Cuba. Castro requested the British and America oil refineries to process the Russian oil. However, the Texas Oil 8F connected oil Refineries in Cuba (Esso, Texaco, Shell) turned down Castro's request to process Russian oil. Castro became angry and nationalized the Cuban Oil Refineries to get his million barrels of oil processed. This enraged the 8F gang that they pushed for sanctions against Castro's Cuba. As a result, Castro kicked out the rest of the US Corporations by Nationalizing them also. Soon, from a minor Socialist state, Cuba developed into full blown Communism and had alliances with Russia in the US's backyard. Matters escalated which finally triggered the Cuban Missile Crisis. The Texas 8F group saw the Cuban Missile Crisis as an opportunity, for dragging the US into a Nuclear War with the Soviet Union, to help bring in the **New World Order**.

The CIA crooks tried to bait John F. Kennedy (JFK) into declaring war on Castro, but he resisted. Instead, JFK used back channel methods to get around the CIA. Then, both he and the Soviet Union's Khrushchev began to gradually untie the knots. The Texas 8F gang and their Royalist pals in Europe consider JFK a threat, for moving toward peace with Russia and Cuba. This Anglo-Zionist group comprising of PERMINDEX, White House Joint Chiefs of Staff, Prince Bernhard's Bilderberg Royals of Europe, Mormon Mafia faction of the CIA, John Birch Society, Oak Ridge nuclear network, UK's Royals, the MOSSAD, J. Edgar Hoover's FBI Division Five Unit, Defense Industrial Security Command (DISC), Meyer Lansky's Jewish dominated Mafia and the Zionist banking elements, then plotted to use their European Intelligence Network to kill JFK in Dallas.

The would-be Dallas JFK killers engaged PERMINDEX political assassin, Major Louis Mortimer Bloomfield, to knock off JFK with foreign drug mafia killers. Corsican killers, like Lucien Sarti, were deadly, guaranteed a Code of silence and took payment in terms of drugs, like Opium. Also, a killing plan that used foreign killers would be harder to investigate and solve, since the killers lived outside the US borders. New Orleans Mafia leader, Carlos Marcello, put out the Mafia solicitations into Marseilles, France, for shooters to kill JFK. Thus, Marcello was acting as a go-between for PERMINDEX represented by Guy Banister and Clay Shaw.

The plot to kill JFK also included the framing of the Soviet Union as the mastermind behind JFK's assassination. Hence, the killing of JFK was also a false flag operation to drag the US into a nuclear war with the Soviet Union. Even before JFK's assassination, H. W. Bush and J. Edgar Hoover decided to use CIA and FBI agent, Lee Harvey Oswald, as a patsy with false links to the KGB. Both H. W. Bush and Edgar Hoover were aware that Oswald belonged to the US patriot faction of American intelligence; and had previously worked as US undercover agent posing as a defector in the Soviet Union. Conspirators of JFK assassination, recruited William Seymour who looked like Lee Harvey Oswald, to plant evidence against Oswald in Mexico, Dallas and New Orleans. In 1962, CIA informant George de Mohrenschildt visited Lee Harvey Oswald and his wife, Marina Oswald, at their home in Fort Worth, Texas. George cultivated a friendship with Oswald. At a party in February 1963, George de Mohrenschildt introduced CIA agent Ruth Paine to both Lee Harvey Oswald and Marina Oswald. Since mid October 1963, Ruth Paine arranged for Lee Harvey Oswald to work at the Texas School Book Depository.

After his return from Russia, Lee Harvey Oswald infiltrated PERMINDEX by working closely with FBI-CIA agent, Guy Bannister, in his detective agency at 544 Camp Street. As a cover for his secret agent identity, Oswald distributed leaflets for the Fair Play For Cuba Committee which was a front for the Mormon Mafia faction of the CIA. Oswald learnt about the plot to assassinate JFK and would update his contacts in the FBI, such as Harry Dean and James P. Hosty. However, Oswald's cover was blown and discovered by Congressman John Rousselot of California and former Army General Edwin A. Walker, both members of the John Birch Society. Thereafter, Oswald was impersonated by William Seymour who made calls to the Soviet Embassy in Mexio City. In one such call, William Seymour referred to a previous meeting with a Soviet official named Kostikov. Expecting his calls to be monitored by the FBI, William knew that the FBI was aware of Kostikov's activities in KGB's "Department 13" involved in sabotage and assassinations. Thus, the idea was to paint Oswald as a hired killer of the Soviet Union. This was the Bolshevik's prescription for World War III.

At the time of JFK assassination, PERMINDEX's Ferenc Nagy lived right in Dallas, Texas, while Clay Shaw lived right in New Orleans with John Birch Society and FBI's Guy Banister who was also a PERMINDEX resource.

In the year 1963, phase two of the Bolshevik Revolution began with the public execution of John F. Kennedy, in the guise of an assassination. Shortly before Kennedy was killed, he announced the withdrawal of all American soldiers from Vietnam by Christmas. Kennedy also called off the invasion of Cuba; and canceled 70 billion dollars in military contracts. Kennedy realized that the CIA was placing the US in grave danger, by acting on their own without the consent or authority of either the president or congress. As such, President Kennedy vowed to splinter the (Zionist-Nazi infiltrated) CIA into a thousand pieces; and scatter it to the winds. As Kennedy had become a threat to the agenda of the Bolsheviks, it was decided that their World Revolution had to be implemented earlier than what was announced by their affiliated British-Israel World Federation in 1922. At the instant of President John F. Kennedy's death, Zionist Jew, Lyndon 'Lyin' Johnson, as he was called, became the unelected President of the United States. Johnson then made it his top priority to immediately reverse several programs initiated by President Kennedy, in accordance to the wishes of the Bolsheviks.

Prescott Bush, Nixon, Vice President Lyndon B. Johnson, Bush Sr. and his Illuminati buddies in the CIA, together with the Jewish dominated Mafia received their orders to kill John F. Kennedy (JFK), from the Bolshevik masterminds such as World Jewish Congress President Nahum Goldmann and Israeli Prime Minister David Ben-Gurion. Lyndon B. Johnson, together with Connally (the governor of Texas) arranged for Abraham Zapruder, a Jew, to stand in exactly the right place for filming the killing of President Kennedy. This was the spot where Mrs. Jacqueline Kennedy would discharge the chamber of a hand gun through her husband's head, as the film taken from the other side of the car from where Abraham Zapruder was positioned, showed. Zapruder's film frame 313 captured the instant of JFK's execution. In fact, the amount and distribution of blood on JFK's shirt revealed that he was shot at point blank range from the lower left side of his head. Jackie Kennedy was the only person who had the access and angle to have delivered the fatal gunshot to JFK. Interestingly, Mrs. Jacqueline Kennedy (Née Bouvier) was a Jewess (and a possible sayanim or Jewish sleeper agent), a fact which her cousin / step-brother, Gore Vidal wrote in his autobiography. Furthermore, Jackie worked for the CIA before marrying JFK. Long before that time, the CIA MK-Ultra (mind control) program already officially began in 1952. Indeed, Jacqueline had also undergone electroshock therapy. It was obvious that Jackie was a programmed 'Monarch slave.' Thus, the Bolsheviks planted persons around Kennedy; and to this day all US Presidents were likewise surrounded by people chosen by the Bolshevik masterminds.

On 22 November 1963, David-ben-Gurion ordered the assassination to remove "an enemy of Israel" went according to the detailed plan that Connally, Johnson and Aristotle Onassis had devised and rehearsed, during the three months that Jacqueline Kennedy was on holiday with Aristotle Onassis (against her husband's wishes). As part of the agreement, Aristotle Onassis married Jacqueline Kennedy after the death of JFK, for the protection of her children and herself.

Secret Purim Celebration At The Bohemian Grove

Before the assassination of JFK, that same year a related event occurred at an exclusive club. On 17 March 1963, a secret gathering was arranged for the celebration of Purim at the Bohemian Grove. Selected high ranking members drove to the 2,700 acre Bohemian Grove, in the dead of night. All these elite members wore black cloaks and masks so that no one knew who were attending. Some elite members were accompanied by scantily clad shapely women who also wore masks.

After showing special passes at the main gate, the guests were led beside a stream to tables and chairs arranged before an altar in front of a huge stone owl.

After most guests were seated, a shofar was blown. There was silence as a man in red cloak and a horned devil mask appeared at the altar. The person with the devil mask gave out a blood curdling shriek and shouted in a deep voice, "Let the worship begin."

Immediately, a blond teenage girl in chains were dragged in front of the alter. The girl was terrified as some of the masked men made her lie upon the altar top. There was applause as the man in the devil mask tore off her clothes.

A group of scantily clad masked women came from among the audience and formed a circle around the altar. They danced around the altar to the sound of a weird satanic music played on an electronic organ. All the while, the naked girl that lay upon the altar squirmed but was unable to stand up and escape.

Suddenly, the music stopped as the man in the devil mask stood in front of the altar with a dagger. He shouted, "We are the immortals, the bloodline of Lilith! This year, we shall carry out a great event at the Pyramid of Dealey Plaza." He continued, "Tonight, blood will be drank as a toast to the next President of the United States of

America." A tall and lanky man wearing a silver face mask stood up at one of the tables; and bowed briefly.

The man with the devil mask, lifted up the dagger, as the naked girl screamed in terror. The dagger was plunged into the heart of the naked girl; and her body went limp. The man with the devil mask proceeded to slit the throat of the girl; and repeatedly stabbed the body at several places. Blood flowed onto the alter; and followed grooves carved onto the surface of the alter. Some of the scantily clad dancers collected the blood with jugs placed at the ends of the grooves.

The man with the devil mask lifted up the mask to expose his cruel thin lips. He took a goblet and collected some of the blood. He then took a sip from the goblet. He commanded, "Pass the drink around." Filled jugs were taken from the alter to the tables; and blood was poured into glasses for the guests.

The lifeless body of the naked girl was thrown into a huge fire that was ignited in front of the stone owl. The charred remains of the girl was then wrapped in plastic sheet and thrown into bushes near the Russian river in Monte Rio, several kilometers from the Bohemian Grove. In mid May 1963, a group of hikers discovered the charred remains. The police from Santa Rosa Police Department then took the remains for analysis by a coroner.

Two months later, a forensic artist reconstructed a face from the skull. At the same time, the coroner determined evidence of stab wounds; and was able to establish that the remains was that of a female teenager. Strands of hair still attached to the skull indicated that the girl was a blond. The dead girl's reconstructed face was then distributed to various police stations, as far away as Arizona.

At that time in Arizona, there were two missing person reports at the police station near Gilbert Arizona. Both persons were teenage girls who were partners of a new boutique shop in Pheonix, Arizona. One of these girls closely resembled the dead girl's reconstructed face.

Hence, it was established that the dead girl could be Jane Field who went missing when she and her partner, Doris Singleton, flew to Las Vegas for the weekend on 15 February 1963.

Trojan Horse Attack At Dealey Plaza

President Kennedy's visit to Texas on 22 November 1963 had been under consideration for almost a year before it occurred. The final decision on the November trip to Texas was made at a meeting between President Kennedy, Vice President Johnson, and Governor Connally on 5 June 1963, at the Cortez Hotel in El Paso, Texas. The three agreed that the President would visit Texas in late November 1963. At the White House, Kenneth O'Donnell, special assistant to the President, acted as coordinator for the Texas trip. A motorcade was planned through downtown Dallas, as the best way for the people to see their President. According to Kenneth O'Donnell, there would always be a motorcade wherever the President went, particularly in large cities, so that the President would be seen by as many people as possible. In O'Donnell's experience, the Secret Service would arrange a route that brought the President through an area which exposes him to the greatest number of people.

An important purpose of the President's visit to Dallas was to speak at a luncheon given by business and civic leaders. Kenneth O'Donnell made the final decision to hold the luncheon at the Trade Mart. 45 minutes had been allotted for a motorcade procession from Love Field airport to the luncheon site of Trade Mart. From Love Field the route passed through a portion of suburban Dallas, through the downtown area along Main Street and then to Trade Mart via Stemmons Freeway. On 14 November 1963, Special Agent Winston G. Lawson, a member of the White House detail, and Forrest V. Sorrels, special agent in charge of the Dallas office, drove over the selected route with Batchelor and other police officers, verifying that it could be traversed within 45 minutes. Representatives of the local host committee and the White House staff were advised by the Secret Service of the actual route on the afternoon of November 18.

The route chosen from the airport to Main Street was the normal one, except where Harwood Street was selected as the means of access to Main Street, in preference to a short stretch of the Central Expressway, which could not accommodate spectators as conveniently as Harwood Street. From Main Street the motorcade turned right at Houston, going one block north and then turning left onto Elm Street. On this last portion of the journey, only 5 minutes from the Trade Mart, the President's motorcade would pass the Texas School Book Depository Building on the northwest corner of Houston and Elm Streets.

As an essential part of the Trojan Horse, Emory P. Roberts assigned seven agents on his shift, namely Sam Kinney, Clint Hill, Paul Landis, William McIntyre, Glen Bennett, George Hickey, and John Ready to the follow-up car. Out of these seven agents, four agents had only hours before participated in heavy drinking at Fort Worth. While leaving Love Field airport on the way to the heart of Dallas, Agent Roberts rose from his seat and, using his voice and several hand gestures, forced agent Henry J. Rybka to fall back from the rear area of JFK's limousine, causing a perplexed Rybka to stop and raise his arms several times in disgust. As a result of the actions of the Trojan Horse team in Dallas, there were no protection on JFK's side of the car (including no bubbletop, partial or full, nor the usual number of motorcycles riding next to JFK), something that occurred everywhere except Dallas.

As JFK's limousine negotiated the 'Pyramid' (street) of Dealey Plaza, all hell broke lose as shots were fired from various positions. Former Secretary of the Navy John B. Connally, Jr. was sitting in the seat in front of JFK (probably because Connally was a known 8F group member and would be a good 'body shield' for JFK). Suddenly, Connally turned around in the Dallas Presidential limousine and uttered some "trigger" code words to Jackie (Jacqueline Bouvier). Just before this, J. F. Kennedy was stunned by a sort of pain, yet the 'bodyguards' who were facing him in the car took no notice. Jackie seemed to be waiting for this effect and was not surprised when he became incapacitated. At this point, Jacqueline Kennedy taking a pistol in her right hand, moved toward JFK. She placed the pistol somewhere below his left ear. At the same time, Lucien Sarti from the Marseilles mob, fired a rifle from behind a picket fence near the Grassy Knoll. Then the 'bodyguards' look the other way, as JFK's head exploded towards the side of the car nearest the Zapruder's camera. During these two fatal shots, the car slowed almost to a halt. The Zapruder's film showed an orange mussel flash coming out of JFK's head followed by his brains. Soon after the simultaneous shots were fired, Jackie crawled onto the trunk of JFK's limousine. Then, the car picked up speed. Later, Jackie admitted that she did not recall that she had crawled onto the car's trunk (typical behaviour of a programmed "sleeper" assassin).

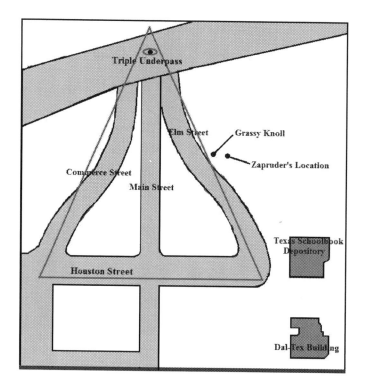

Pyramid Of Dealey Plaza

Other shots were fired at JFK's limousine. A shot fired from the storm drain wounded John Connally. By that time, Jackie had already crawled onto the trunk of the car; and no bullet hit her.

Tying Up Loose Ends

The Bolsheviks immediately cover up their tracks before, during and after JFK's assassination.

As shots were fired at JFK, Lee Harvey Oswald (LHO) had already left the Texas School Book Depository Building. Oswald decided to watch a movie because he expected no more work that afternoon. Unknown to him, a contract was out to kill him at about the same time that killers were shooting at JFK. The hired killers became desperate because they could not find Oswald at his place of work. In an attempt to create an alternative script, a conspirator of the JFK assassination, George H. W. Bush, 5535 Briar, Houston, telephoned the FBI Houston office that one James Parrott had been talking of killing President Kennedy when he comes to Houston.

Mafia bribed police officers and hired killers made a frantic joint search for Oswald. One of the hired killers, a stocky Latino-looking man with dark wavy hair and tan jacket, drove Mrs. Paine's Rambler station wagon to pick up DISC agent, William Seymour, near the Dealey Plaza. The Rambler station wagon then sped towards the area at Oak Cliff. At about 1:15pm, police officer, Jefferson David Tippit, was cruising east in his patrol car on 10th Street. A hundred feet past the intersection with Patton Avenue, Tippet stopped William Seymour who walked briskly looking for Oswald, east along the south side of Patton Avenue. William approached the police patrol car; and exchanged words with Tippit through the right window. Tippit stepped out of the car and began to walk round towards the front of the car. Suddenly, William produced a revolver and fired several shots at officer Tippit who died on the spot.

Finally, the Mafia bribed police officers located Oswald in a movie theatre; and prepared an ambush to kill Oswald in an alley behind the theatre. However, a man named Brewer saw Oswald went into the theater without buying a ticket. Brewer alerted the woman in the box office to call police. Brewer then told his suspicions to the concessions operator; and the two stood by the emergency exits. Upon hearing a noise behind his alley-exit door, Brewer opened the door, only to have police guns aimed at him. The movie theater lights were then switched on. Brewer pointed out the suspicious man seated in the theater. Oswald was arrested after a brief scuffle, during which he punched an officer and pulled a gun. Before he could fire a shot, Oswald was overpowered by the police. Unknown to Oswald, someone had removed the firing pin of his revolver. Hence, it was fortunate that Oswald did not pull the trigger. Oswald was taken to the police station. There, he was initially questioned by police officers, Guy F. Rose and Richard S. Stovall. Oswald was further interrogated at the office of Capt. Will Fritz. During the interrogation, Oswald seemed to know that both JFK and police officer, Jefferson Davis Tippit, were killed. Still, he denied any involvement in the shootings.

The original plan to kill Oswald at the Texas School Book Depository Building failed. The script had to be changed at the last minute. Hence, the plot to blame JFK's assassination on the Soviet Union was aborted. Still, Oswald had to be silenced. On 11:21am, Sunday, 24 November 1963, Jewish mobster and FBI informant, Jack Ruby (aka Jacob Leon Rubenstein) shot dead LHO, as instructed by FBI-CIA agent, Guy Bannister. In helping the Anglo-Zionists to eliminate a loose end, both Guy Banister and Jack Ruby also became loose ends. In June 1964, Guy Bannister (Jack's contact to PERMINDEX) died of an induced heart attack. By 3 January 1967, Jack was killed with a biological agent (courtesy of CIA linked killing unit called BP-7), at Dallas Parkland Memorial Hospital.

After dark on 24 November 1963, George Senator was interviewed by newsmen, in the presence of his friend, Jim Martin, and his Attorney, Tom Howard, at Jack Ruby's apartment in Oak

Cliff. The newsmen were Bill Hunter of the Long Beach California Press Telegram and Jim Koethe of the Dallas Times Herald. At that time, George Senator was Jack Ruby's roommate. In the same night of the interview, newsman Bill Hunter was shot. A few months after Hunter's death, Lawyer Tom Howard was observed to be acting strangely by his friends, two days later Tom died of an induced heart attack. On 21 September 1964, just as Jim Koethe, of the Dallas Times Herald, emerged from a shower in his apartment, an intruder attacked him with a karate chop to the throat. Jim died instantly.

Dorothy Kilgallen was the only journalist who was granted a private interview with Jack Ruby after he killed Lee Harvey Oswald. Judge Joe B. Brown granted the interview during the course of the Ruby trial in Dallas. Apparently, Miss Kilgallen paid much money to Judge Brown, for the favor. In her euphoria, Miss Kilgallen stated that she was "going to break this case wide open." On 8 November 1965, Miss Kilgallen was murdered. Chemical analysis of the glass Kilgallen had been drinking from when she died, showed traces of a sedative called Nembutol. Yet, Nembutol was not found in her blood. Instead, the blood tests turned up a lethal cocktail of drugs: secobarbitol, amobarbital and pentobarbital. Two days later, a close friend of Miss Kilgallen's, Mrs. Earl T. Smith, died of undetermined causes.

Lee Bowers was one of the 65 witnesses who saw the President's assassination. He thought shots were fired from the area of the Grassy Knoll (The Knoll is west of the Texas School Book Depository Building). During the assassination, Bowers, then a towerman for the Union Terminal Co., was stationed in his 14 foot tower directly behind the Grassy Knoll. He faced the scene of the assassination. Directly in front of him was a parking lot and a wooden stockade fence, and a row of trees running along the top of the Grassy Knoll. The Knoll sloped down to the spot on Elm Street where the President was killed. Bowers observed two unfamiliar men standing on the top of the Knoll at the edge of the parking lot, within 10 or 15 feet of each other. When shots rang out, Bowers's attention was drawn to the area where he had seen the two men. Bowers testified that the "commotion" that caught his eye may have been a "flash of light or smoke." On the morning of August 9, 1966, Lee Bowers was driving south of Dallas on business. He was two miles south of Midlothian, Texas when his brand **new** company car veered from the road and hit a bridge abutment. Bowers died in a Dallas hospital. There was no autopsy and he was cremated. A doctor from Midlothian who rode to Dallas in the ambulance with Bowers, said, "He was in some strange sort of shock. A different kind of shock than an accident victim experiences. I can't explain it. I've never seen anything like it." Bowers's widow later said, "They told him not to talk."

More than a hundred witnesses to the JFK assassination, died mysteriously. The Bolsheviks were determined that there would be no loose ends.

Birth Of A Vampire Killer

Sergeant Edward Field from Dallas Police Department, Texas, had not heard from his sister, Jane Field, since mid February 1963. Edward's sister, Jane, had called him on 15 February 1963. She told him that she would be going to Las Vegas with her partner, Doris Singleton, for a weekend holiday.

On 18 July 1963, Sergeant Edward Field called Jane's boutique shop situated in Phoenix, Arizona. There was no response. Instead, a recorded message from an operator informed that the number was discontinued.

Sergeant Edward Field was worried, but he was soon engaged in several homicide cases which kept him occupied. However, on 12 August 1963, Edward decided to take a one week leave to visit Jane in Phoenix, Arizona. Approval for leave was granted; and Edward took a flight from Dallas, Fort Worth to Phoenix, Arizona, on Sunday, 25 August 1963.

Upon reaching Phoenix at noon, Edward hailed a cab to his sister's rented apartment, called Monterra Apartments at 1333 North 24th St. Phoenix AZ 85008. It was Sunday and Edward thought that his sister would be home from church. When Edward reached his sister's apartment, no one answered the door. A neighbor confirmed that two teenage girls lived in the apartment, but went missing. The local police had been at the apartment and found the girls' belongings still inside the apartment.

Edward hurried to the Pheonix Police Department. After introducing himself, a police officer told Edward that he recalled a missing girl with the same surname as Edward's. Later, Edward was shown the reconstructed face of Jane Field. Edward's heart sank because he immediately recognized his sister.

Jane's friend, Doris Singleton, was still not found. Edward decided to follow the lead and go to Las Vegas immediately. Edward knew Doris Singleton and had a photo taken of Jane and Doris, before they left for Pheonix, Arizona, in early 1962. Edward managed to take a night flight from Pheonix, Arizona, to Las Vegas, Nevada. Edward booked into the DoubleTree by Hilton Hotel Las Vegas Airport. He decided to stay for the night and move around Las Vegas in the following morning.

Edward had a sleepless night. He tossed and turned, blaming himself for not being by Jane's side when she needed him most. Edward knew that he had to pull himself together and find his sister's killers.

The next day, Edward checked out of the hotel and moved around Las Vegas. He had to seek help in locating Doris Singleton, if she was still alive. It was noon and Edward had shown the photo of Jane and Doris to numerous passersby. Edward decided to book into a cheap hotel room and call his colleagues in Dallas Police Department, Texas. One of Edward's colleagues suggested him to look up a private detective friend called Thomas Kindle. Edward obtained the address of Thomas Kindle's private detective agency, he took a cab and reached the office of Thomas Kindle.

Thomas Kindle had a shabby small office with enough room for a desk and some filing cabinets. There were many piles of documents stacked on the floor and the desk. Edward introduced himself to Thomas Kindle who was heavy built with the look of a wrestler. Thomas was already expecting Edward because Edward's colleague had just called in. Thomas immediately speculated that the Mafia was involved. Both men went around Las Vegas and talked to some usual informants of Thomas. It was well known that Las Vegas was a centre for money laundering. Therefore, there would be many crimes committed, for 'dirty' money to be laundered at the Casinos. In the case of the missing girls, Thomas guessed that they could be kidnapped by the mob for prostitution. After several hours, there were no leads.

Edward and Thomas had a late lunch; and continued their search. This time, Thomas took Edward around several cab companies, in the hope that the girls took cabs while they were in Las Vegas. Unfortunately, there were still no leads.

It was late in the afternoon, both Edward and Thomas dropped into a small pub at South Las Vegas Boulevard, for a drink. As they were drinking beer, Thomas noticed a pimp whom he knew. "Come here," Thomas ordered the pimp. The pimp who looked like a scarecrow, took hesitant steps towards Thomas and Edward. "Saw these girls," Thomas nodded to Edward who showed the pimp the photo of Jane and Doris. The pimp's face beamed, as he took a close look at the photo. "I've seen one of them," said the pimp, "How much am I gonna be paid?"

Edward handed a ten dollar note to the pimp. "There's more if you can take us to see her," said Edward. The pimp nodded and he went with Thomas and Edward. The pimp pointed out the way, as

Thomas drove his car towards the Western side of Las Vegas. They reached a huge mansion with a cast iron gate. The mansion looked deserted with fungus growing on the walls.

"Give me the money," said the nervous pimp, "I want to be back in town." Edward handed another ten dollar note to the pimp while Thomas drove back to the pub. As the pimp got off the car, Thomas warned him, "I'll be back, if you lied!"

It was dusk when Thomas dropped Edward back at the cheap hotel. Edward arranged for Thomas to pick him up the next morning.

Edward had a light meal at the hotel cafeteria. He went straight to bed after dinner. It was midnight when Edward suddenly woke up. The room was filled with the odor of rotten flesh. Edward pinched himself to make sure that he was awake. Cold sweat poured down his face as he felt an eerie presence. A tall figure in black cloak stepped out of the shadows in his room.

Edward froze in bed. As the intruder approached Edward's bed, he could make out the ashen face of a man. Edward reached out for his revolver and pointed it at the man. In the twinkle of an eye, the figure merged back into the shadows. Edward could sense that he was now alone again. The strange odor was also gone!

Edward did not sleep well after the episode in the room. The next morning, he got up early and waited for Thomas to pick him up. When Thomas showed up, they quickly proceeded to head for the old mansion. Edward decided not to tell Thomas of his encounter during the night.

When Thomas and Edward reached the old mansion, it still looked deserted. Thomas got out of his car and shouted, "Is anyone around?" Suddenly, an old caretaker appeared at the cast iron gate. The caretaker said in a gruff voice, "My master will not see anyone."

Edward introduced himself, "Sergeant Edward Field from Dallas Police Department, Texas." The caretaker hesitated and said, "Wait awhile." Then the caretaker hurried back into the mansion. A few minutes later, the caretaker emerged from the mansion and said, "My master shall see you this afternoon at 3:00pm."

Thomas drove Edward back to town for lunch. After lunch, Edward dozed off in his chair. At 2:00pm, Thomas shook Edward awake. "Tired?" Thomas asked with a grin. Thomas then drove Edward to the old mansion.

Thomas and Edward were shown into a musty hall. As they sat on a sofa, a couple walked into the room. The man looked middle age and introduced himself as Benjamin Scull. Edward looked at the face of a smiling woman who was accompanying the man. "Hello Edward," she greeted him. Edward recognized her to be Doris Singleton.

Edward asked Doris, "What happened?" Doris replied, "I am staying with Benjamin, my fiancé. Your sister is now staying with friends in San Francisco." Edward knew that Doris was lying because Jane was already dead.

Edward controlled himself and requested Doris to give him Jane's address and contact telephone. Doris replied, "I am happy to oblige, but first, why don't you come for dinner with your friend, tonight?" Edward agreed and left with Thomas, to the pub at South Las Vegas Boulevard.

It was 7:00pm when Edward and Thomas returned to the mansion. The caretaker was not around, but the cast iron gate was opened. Thomas drove past the gate and parked his car near the front porch of the old mansion. Near the front door of the mansion stood a tall man in black suit. As Edward and Thomas approached him, he said, "Master is waiting."

Edward and Thomas were shown into a dimly lit dining room. As they sat at the dining table, they were joined by Benjamin and Doris. Soon, the dinner started, but no one said a word.

After dinner, everyone went into an adjourning room for drinks. Suddenly, a weird organ music filled the room. Edward and Thomas felt nauseating. Edward could feel the presence of other people in the room. The lights in the room went dim; and out of the shadows hooded figures appeared. They were chanting. Edward looked around for Thomas, but he could not find him. Edward was now afraid. It appeared that he was in the middle of a ritual.

Edward bolted across the room and went out the door. He tried his best to head for the main door of the mansion. A dark figure darted after Edward. Edward felt that something he ate or drank was affecting him. Edward was slowing down, but he knew that he must continue moving.

Just as Edward was approaching the front door of the mansion, he stumbled. The dark figure caught up with Edward and stood over him. Edward rolled over and looked up. He could make out the same ashen face of the intruder who visited him the previous night.

The creature snarled at Edward. Adrenaline was pumping through Edward. With his heart pounding, Edward reached out for his revolver and shot the thing between the eyes.

Edward got up and made his way out of the front door. He ran past the parked car of Thomas; and out through the cast iron gate. There were screams of a crowd of people chasing Edward who continued to run. Edward was confused and frightened. It was pitch black as he ran past fields and trees. Finally, Edward stumbled on a broken branch and rolled down a slope. Then, darkness came over Edward; and he passed out.

2

The Epic Of Lilith

Early next morning, Edward stirred at the bottom of a slope. Edward's head was swimming; and he felt weak. Edward staggered up the slope, to find out where he was. At the top of the slope, Edward spotted the old mansion about one kilometer away.

Slowly, Edward made his way to the old mansion. When he reached the mansion, there was nobody in sight, but the cast iron gate was shut. Edward climbed over the gate and walked towards the mansion. At the front porch, Thomas's car was no longer there. The whole place seemed deserted.

Edward tried the front door, it opened easily. Inside, there was no one. At a corridor, Edward saw the portrait of a sinister looking woman, with blood dripping down from the corners of her lips. On the woman's shoulder sat an owl. Edward noticed that this woman bore some resemblance to Doris.

Edward left the mansion; and decided to head for the city area. He hiked part of the way; and hitched a ride from a passing van. By the time Edward reached the city, it was way past noon. Edward headed for the small pub at South Las Vegas Boulevard where he drank a beer and had a light meal. After lunch, Edward took a cab to Thomas Kindle's private detective agency. The door of the agency was ajar; and the whole office was a mess.

Edward looked at some documents strewn across the table and the floor. There were no new information that he could gather. Edward left the office and proceeded to check out of the cheap hotel. As his hotel room's intruder was associated with the group from the old mansion. Edward reasoned that he must take precautions.

Edward rented a car and drove to the small pub at South Las Vegas Boulevard, but he did not enter the pub. Instead, he parked the car a few blocks away and waited to spot the pimp. It was almost dark, when Edward saw the pimp walked into the pub. After half an hour, the pimp emerged in the company of a burly man. Edward tailed both men, as they walked down the Strip towards the Riviera hotel. Then, both men turned left into Riviera Boulevard.

A car picked up the two men at Riviera Boulevard. Edward then tailed the car which finally reached a large residential building in Regatta Drive. Edward saw the pimp, the burly man and two other men alight from the car; and they entered the building.

Edward parked the car and followed. He could see that the front door of the building was opened. Edward stepped inside, into a lobby where a huge wooden carving of an owl stood at a corner. Some voices above him attracted Edward to a flight of steps leading upstairs.

Edward darted up the stairs. At the top of the stairs, Edward saw a long corridor. There were voices coming from a room to the left of the corridors. The door to that room was opened and Edward managed to make out what was said. ". . . You showed a police officer to our master's home." "I was careless," pleaded the pimp, "it will never happen again." "Where is the police officer?" asked another man. The pimp said, "he checked out of the hotel this afternoon." A low menacing voice said, "we must cover our tracks. No one should be able to find out about Operation Bay Of Pigs Redacted." Suddenly, Edward heard two muffled gun shots. The pimp gasped, "No . . ." Another muffled shot was fired; and then there was silence.

Edward stealthily darted down the stairs. In a flash, Edward drove away in his car. He had some good leads, but he needed to leave Las Vegas immediately. Edward returned the rented car at the airport. He then purchased a ticket to Phoenix, Arizona. That night, Edward reached Pheonix, Arizona.

The next day, Edward went to the Pheonix Police Department. He requested the remains of his sister, Jane Field. The Pheonix Police Department called the Santa Rosa Police Department; and informed them about Jane's next-of-kin, Sergeant Edward Field. The Pheonix Police Department also handed over the girls' belongings from the Pheonix apartment to Edward. Edward immediately packed the belongings for delivery to his home at Dallas Texas. Then, he took a flight from Pheonix, Arizona, to Santa Rosa Sonoma County airport. There, he took a taxi to Santa Rosa Police Department where he collected the frozen remains of his sister.

Burial Of A Vampire Victim

Edward prepared his sister's burial, as soon as he reached Dallas, Texas. Only Edward's colleagues and some of his close relatives attended the funeral.

Edward stayed back at his sister's grave, after everyone had left. Thoughts of his happier childhood days and moments with his sister, flashed through his mind. Edward now knew that Doris Singleton was complicit in his sister's murder. He resolved to find out all he could about Doris.

Back at home, Edward drew a simple chart on a piece of paper. On the chart, Edward indicated that Doris Singleton was linked to an unknown occult group. Edward also noted the address of the large residential building in Regatta Drive, as belonging to the occult group. Edward made a note that Benjamin Scull was the leader of the occult group. Other notes were written on the chart, such as the owl symbol, the area near the Russian river where Jane's body was found and an operation known as 'The Bay of Pigs Redacted.'

Several days later, Edward received the belongings of Jane and Doris, through parcel mail. He examined the items in the parcel and came across Jane's photo album. As Edward reviewed the photos, he saw a photo of Jane when she was a school girl with another girl who resembled Doris. Both girls wore the same school uniforms. Hence, Edward concluded that Jane knew Doris since they were classmates.

The next day, Edward applied leave for another week. The Dallas Police Department approved Edward's leave application based on compassionate grounds. That afternoon, Edward went to his sister's former school, to see the principal. The principal supplied Edward with Doris's home address. Edward saw Doris's aged mother still living at the address; and they had tea. During their conversation, Edward learnt that Doris's parents were Russian Jews who migrated to the US, before the Bolshevik revolution. Edward asked whether the aged lady had heard of Doris's fiancé, Benjamin Scull. Doris's mother did not seem to be aware that Doris was engaged. However, she informed Edward, that Doris was active in the B'nai B'rith youth movement at Northaven Road, Dallas, Texas. Perhaps, Doris met her fiancé there.

Next morning, Edward made his way to the B'nai B'rith youth organization at 7900 Northaven Road, Dallas. Edward found that the organization promoted charity, social networking and informal teaching of the Halakha which was the Jewish Oral law. Edward used Doris's missing person status as his reason for searching someone in the organization who knew Doris. Finally, Edward discovered that Doris used to network with a group that studied the Kabbalah. Edward then obtained the names of some members of this group.

Edward went to bookshops to search for books on the Kabbalah. In one of the books, it was written that the Kabbalah was the foundation of modern witchcraft. Edward then learnt that a famous witch called Helena Petrovna Blavatsky (1831-1891) introduced a type of spiritualism borrowed from Hindu mysticism and the Jewish Kabbalah which she defined as 'Theosophy.' Edward concluded that Doris was involved in occult practice with a Jewish group. Thus, he decided to find out more about the Kabbalah and witchcraft. On Monday 9 September 1963, Edward's enquiries, on the subject of the Kabbalah and witchcraft, led him to the University of North Texas where there was a Jewish studies program. Edward met the lecturer of Jewish studies, Mr. Clive Barker, who told him that the Kabbalah was Jewish mysticism derived from the Babylonian Talmud.

Edward invited Mr. Clive Barker for coffee. While they were having coffee, Clive explained to Edward that the Babylonian Talmud was the holy book of Judaism. Edward wanted to know more about the Kabbalah and witchcraft. Clive told Edward that the Kabbalah originated from the 'initiated' Talmudists. The two chief classics of the Kabbalah, were the Jetzirah and the Zohar which formed the basis of an occult religion. Thus, the Kabbalah was a branch of Jewish mysticism which began about the 13th Century. Freemasonry was derived from the Kabbalah. An offshoot of Freemasonry was the Ordo Templi Orientis (the Oriental Order of the Templars). The famous wizard, Aleister Crowley, was a Grand Master of the Ordo Templi Orientis in Britain and Ireland. Hence, witchcraft could be traced to the Kabbalah.

Edward asked Clive about the totem of the owl. Clive informed that the owl often represented Lilith who was in fact, the Babylonian goddess Semiramis. The cult of Lilith was associated with sacred sex and temple prostitution. In Jewish mythology, Lilith was the first wife of Adam. She left Adam, so God created Eve. Eve mated with Adam and gave birth to the common people in the world. On the other hand, Lilith mated with demons; and gave birth to demonic beings who were killed by God's angels. Lilith then stole some of the children whom she killed by drinking their blood. Thus, Lilith became the first vampire in the world. She was described as a screeching owl who murdered infants and tormented lonely men at night—the original succubus. Two organizations that used initiations and magic associated with Lilith would be the Ordo Antichristianus Illuminati and the Order of Phosphorus. Clive added that Lilith was the demonic goddess of the Bohemian Grove located at 20601 Bohemian Avenue, in Monte Rio, California. Edward immediately sat up and realized there could be a connection with the location of Jane's body.

Visit Of A Vampire

It was getting dark, by the time Edward returned home. Edward had a lot to think about.

After a quick meal, Edward took out the chart that he had prepared several days ago. Using this original chart, Edward prepared a new chart on a fresh piece of paper. In the new chart, Edward linked Doris Singleton to a Jewish Kabbalistic group. He made a note that the owl symbol was related to the worship of Lilith. Edward also noted that the Russian river was in the vicinity of Bohemian Grove. As Edward continued to look at the original chart, he thought that the operation 'The Bay of Pigs Redacted' sounded familiar. Still, he could not yet figure out why the operation sounded so familiar. Edward filed the two pieces of paper in a new folder. He then took a bottle of beer from the fridge and watched television.

Edward dozed off in front of the television. Edward woke up to the sound of the doorbell. He switched off the television and staggered to the front door. Edward opened the door and saw a tall young man with blood shot eyes.

The young man politely introduced himself as Joseph Baren. Joseph was well dressed in a dark suit; and asked permission to have a few words with Edward.

Edward invited the young man to step into his living room. Once they were seated, Joseph told Edward that he was a cousin of Doris; and was aware that Edward was looking for her.

Edward told Joseph that he was seeking Doris because she was the last person with his sister, Jane, who was murdered. Joseph expressed condolence on Jane's demise. However, Edward could tell that Joseph was not sincere.

Edward asked Joseph about his present employment. Joseph told Edward that he worked at J. P. Morgan Chase Bank in Dallas, Texas. Edward then offered Joseph a drink before they continue with the conversation. Joseph requested some Brandy. Edward excused himself and went into the kitchen, to pour Brandy for himself and Joseph. As he was pouring Brandy, Edward felt the presence of Joseph standing behind him. It was an eerie feeling.

"Nice kitchen," said Joseph. Edward turned around; and offered a glass of Brandy to Joseph.

Both men toasted and sipped Brandy. "Perhaps, you could let me know the purpose of your visit?" asked Edward.

"Just getting acquainted with you," said Joseph who stared at Edward with his bloodshot eyes.

Edward felt Joseph's stare was hypnotic; and looked away. "It is getting late, I must go now," apologized Joseph.

Edward showed Joseph to the front door. As soon as the door was opened, Joseph melted into the night. Edward peered out into his front lawn, but there was no trace of Joseph. Edward felt spooky.

Edward looked at the wall clock which showed 1:00am in the morning. Realizing it was late, Edward went to his upstairs bedroom. Very soon he was sound asleep in bed.

In his sleep, Edward dreamt that he was walking past the opened cast iron gates, in front of the huge mansion in Las Vegas. Mist was everywhere. Suddenly, Edward heard the overhead flutter of wings.

He looked up and saw an owl hovered above him. The owl swooped down and turned into a maiden wearing a scarlet dress. Edward peered at the maiden and recognized the face of Doris. Then the maiden vaporized and Edward was alone again.

The Kabbalah, Bohemian Grove And Operation Bay Of Pigs

The next day, Edward woke up with memories of the mysterious night visitor and the haunting dream of Doris still fresh in his mind. He felt very strongly that Jane's death was the work of a Jewish Kabbalah group. Hence, Edward decided to locate two of Doris's previous friends from the Kabbalah study group at B'nai B'rith youth organization. Edward chose to find Benjamin Charog first.

Edward went to the Jewish Federation Of Greater Dallas which was a synagogue near the B'nai B'rith Youth Organization. He found out that Benjamin Charog sometimes attended service, at that synagogue. Someone from the synagogue told Edward that Benjamin Charog was working at Goldman Sachs Bank in Dallas, Texas. Edward paid a visit to the Goldman Sachs Bank at 100 Crescent Court, Suite 1000 Dallas, Texas. Benjamin Charog was a senior accountant at Goldman Sachs Bank. Edward introduced himself as a friend of Doris. As it was close to lunch time, Benjamin invited Edward to a nearby cafeteria. Benjamin told Edward that they would be joined by someone from the Crescent Court Branch of the JP Morgan Chase Bank.

Edward asked Benjamin if he had some recent news about Doris. Before Benjamin could answer, Joseph Baren joined them. This time Joseph Baren did not have bloodshot eyes. It was a complete surprise to Edward who informed Benjamin that he had already met Joseph.

Benjamin told Edward that he did not keep in touch with people from the B'nai B'rith youth organization for many years. Joseph said that he knew Benjamin after they met at a banking seminar one year ago. Still, Edward thought that it was such a coincidence for both Joseph and Benjamin to know Doris.

Edward asked if any of them had heard of the Bohemian Grove. Both men looked at each other; and then gazed at Edward as though he had just said something unspeakable. There was a long silence. Finally, Benjamin informed that it was a secret club for the elite. Both men excused themselves and left Edward sitting alone. Edward realized that he had to find out more about the Bohemian Grove.

Next, Edward looked up Miriam Zadok who worked in a news company called Texas Observer, located at 307 West 7th Street Austin, Texas. According to Miriam, she last heard from Doris when she and a friend called Jane accompanied some rich Texas oil tycoon to Del Charro Hotel in California for a holiday, in January 1963.

To Edward, this was a new clue. He knew that Jane would not have the connection with any rich oilman from Texas. Edward guessed that it would be Doris with such a connection.

Edward was eager to learn more, so he invited Miriam for dinner. During dinner, Edward asked Miriam about the Bohemian Grove. Miriam explained that it was a secret club for influential people such as politicians and leaders of the 'Military-industrial complex.' Miriam added that some regular guests of the Del Charro Hotel, were also members of the Bohemian Grove.

Edward wanted more information about the Kabbalah, but Miriam informed him that she was no longer involved. However, Miriam told Edward that Doris belonged to an ancient family tree of Kabbalists.

Edward was happy to have met Miriam because she was helpful. Edward thought about his experience at Las Vegas, he speculated that the pimp was associated with the Mafia mob. Thus, he guessed that the burly man and his companions whom he tailed to Regatta

Drive in Las Vegas, were Mafia members. Since Miriam was in the news business, Edward asked her if she was aware that the Mafia was involved in an operation known as 'The Bay Of Pigs.'

Miriam was amused and she commented that the Bay of Pigs operation was an unsuccessful military action in Cuba by a paramilitary group, in April 1961. The paramilitary group was trained and funded by the CIA, as part of the policy of US President Dwight D. Eisenhower who wanted to overthrow Cuban Prime Minister Fidel Castro. Suddenly, Edward realized why operation 'Bay of Pigs Redacted' sounded so familiar. Still, he doubted that the Mafia would plan another attempt to overthrow Fidel Castro. At the same time, Edward was curious about the connection between the Kabbalah and the Mafia.

Edward decided to go to the University of North Texas the next day; and see Clive Barker.

Back home, Edward drew a fresh chart on a clean sheet of paper, based on new information about Doris. On the new chart, Edward linked Doris to an unknown Texan Oilman, the Del Charro Hotel and the Bohemian Grove. Edward also linked the Mafia to operation 'Bay of Pigs Redacted.'

The next day, Edward called Clive to make an appointment. Clive was free in the morning, so Edward immediately drove to the University of North Texas.

Edward was shown to Clive's office. In the office, Edward asked Clive about the connection between the Mafia and the Kabbalah. Clive informed that the Mafia was set up by an occult organization called the Bavarian Illuminati. The Bavarian Illuminati was organized on 1 May 1776, under Jesuit orders, by a Jew named Adam Weishaupt. In 1834, Giuseppe Mazzini of Italy, a 33rd degree Mason, replaced Adam Weishaupt as the head of the Illuminati. Mazzini created the Mafia's blood rituals and secret oathes. He gave the 'Cosa Nostra,' the name 'MAFIA.' MAFIA is an acronym for Mazzini, Autorizza, Furti, Incendi and Avvelengmenti (in English it meant "Mazzini Authorizes Theft, Arson and Poisoning"). Known as the Mafiosi, they were authorized by Mazzini to commit thefts, arson and murder. The Mafia arrived on American shores in the 1890's with funds from the Illuminati, to establish underground networks and the Black market system. Notorious American Mafiosi were men like Lucky Luciano and Al Capone. The crimes of the American Mafiosi was a window to the type of activities that the current Illuminati conducted through world governments, on a 'legitimate' basis.

Clive stated that the Illuminati are the heirs to the Kabbalistic tradition because the family of Rothschild is one of a cabal of 13 immensely powerful Satanist families. It was in 1775 that at the behest of Meyer Rothschild, Weishaupt began to organize the Illuminati. The first chapter of the order started in Weishaupt's home town of Ingolstadt.

Edward wanted to know the connection between the Mafia and operation 'Bay of Pigs.' Clive suggested that his colleague called Grant Thomson who specializes in Political Science would be in a better position to help him. Clive then took Edward and introduced him to Grant Thomson in the next office.

Grant Thomson was free in the afternoon. Both Edward and Grant went to the University cafeteria for a simple lunch. As they were having lunch, Edward asked Grant about the involvement of the Mafia in operation 'Bay of Pigs.' Grant said that oil companies would tend to be involve in operation 'Bay of Pigs' because Castro nationalized the Cuban Oil Refineries. The Mafia would also tend to be involve in operation 'Bay of Pigs' because Castro closed down the casinos.

After lunch, Edward followed Grant back to his office. Grant then proceeded to brief about the role of Texan oilmen in US politics.

Long before 1953, George H. W. Bush (Bush Sr.) and Thomas J. Devine were oil-wildcatting associates—they explored oil wells drilled in areas not known to be oilfields. In 1953, Zapata Oil was founded by Bush Sr., John Overbey, Hugh Liedtke, Bill Liedtke and Thomas J. Devine. At that time, both Bush Sr. and Thomas Devine were working for the CIA under commercial cover. In 1958, there were drilling contracts with the seven large US oil producers (aka the "Seven Sisters"), included wells 40 miles (64 km) north of Isabela, Cuba. In January 1959, the Cuban government of Fulgencio Batista was overthrown in a Cuban Revolution. US President Dwight Eisenhower was concerned with Cuba's development of strong ties with the Soviet Union. In March 1960, Eisenhower gave US$13 million to the CIA, to plan the overthrow of Cuban leader, Castro. The CIA organized a Cuban invasion, with the aid of the Texan oilmen, Mafia and Cuban counter-revolutionary forces.

Grant paused and gathered his thoughts before continuing, he told Edward that "Operation Zapata" was the codename for the Bay of Pigs military campaign. In fact, the CIA used companies like Zapata to stage and supply secret missions attacking Fidel Castro's Cuban government in advance of the Bay of Pigs invasion. During this invasion, Zapata Off-Shore even provided two of the smaller ships (called Barbara J and Houston). Hence, oilman Bush Sr.'s involvement in the Cuban invasion was obvious because he named the ship, USS San Jacinto, on which he served during WWII as "Barbara" while Bush Sr.'s hometown was Houston, Texas.

The most prominent Texas oilmen were mostly conservative businessmen like H. L. Hunt, Clint Murchison, Wofford Cain and D. H. "Dry Hole" Byrd. On the other hand, the wilder Sid Richardson of Fort Worth was also considered a prominent Texas oilman. These men went to work when oil was first discovered in the early part of the twentieth century; and when the "black giant" was discovered in their back yards in 1931, they moved into part of east Texas which extended over five counties. During these early years, a close relationship developed between Big Oil and Washington.

Hence, nationalization of the Cuban Oil Refineries by Castro, was considered an economic attack against Washington.

When Castro took over Cuba from dictator Battista, he destroyed the lucrative Mafia gambling empire run for Onassis, by Jewish mobster, Meyer Lansky. Castro scoops up US6$ million in Mafia casino receipts. Onassis was a Greek drug pusher and ship owner, who in 1932, partnered with Joseph Kennedy, Eugene Meyer and Meyer Lansky in profitable booze and heroin trades. In 1934, Aristotle Onassis had an oil transportation agreement with Rockefeller and the Seven Sisters (major oil companies). In September 1957, Onassis announced to US Mafia heads, his game plan for acquiring power, by buying US senators, congressmen, judges, governors, to take legal control of the US government.

Edward thanked Grant for his information on Big Oil, Mafia and politics. Edward concluded that the central figure in Big Oil, Mafia and politics was a little known person called Aristotle Onassis. Edward felt overwhelmed by so much information in one day; and needed time to reflect on what he had learnt with respect to his investigations on his sister's murder.

The London Connection, Del Charro Hotel Guests And The Mob

As he drove home from the University of North Texas, Edward noticed that his car was being followed. Edward continued on his way until he reached the shop where he usually bought his household supplies. Edward parked nearby and entered the shop. Then he asked permission from the grocer, to exit through the back door. As they knew each other, the grocer agreed to the request.

Behind the shop, Edward found a narrow path which led to the main road where his car was parked. From behind some bushes, Edward saw the other car that was tailing him. Two men were inside the car; and they were watching the shop. Furtively, Edward crept closer until he could see the car's license plate. He took down the number and called his colleagues at the police station to make a check on the car. Edward also arranged an ambush for the strangers inside the car. Edward stealthily walked back to the shop through the narrow path and exited out of the shop's front door. Then, Edward returned to his car and drove to a road near the police station. Occasionally, Edward would make sure that the other car was still following.

As soon as Edward reached the road near the police station, there was a burst of sirens. Police cars appeared out of nowhere and surrounded the car that was tailing Edward. The two men in the other car, meekly surrendered, then allowed themselves to be searched and handcuffed. At the police station, Edward joined in the interrogation of the men. One man carried the identification of a CIA agent named Jack Smith while the other man was a drug trafficker and mobster, by the name of Rudy Bicciato. Edward was astounded that a CIA agent would be associated with an underworld figure. Both men were silent when asked about their reason for following Edward. The police decided to lock them up for the night and investigate further in the morning. Edward was excited because the next day would be his first day of work after his one week leave.

At home, Edward made a new chart before he went to bed. In this chart, he linked Doris to the Kabbalah; and the Kabbalah to the Bohemian Grove. Then, Edward also linked the Kabbalah to the Illuminati which he then linked to the Rothschild family. Edward also linked the Mafia to the Illuminati. Then he wrote the term 'Bay of Pigs' which he linked to Cuba; and Edward noted that Texan oilmen, the Mafia, CIA and Aristotle Onassis were all involved in the Bay of Pigs operation. He had a hunch that his sister's death was related to operation 'Bay of Pigs Redacted.'

Next morning, 12 September 1963, Edward reported for duty. He was eager to interrogate the two men who were arrested last night. Before he could see the two men, his superior, Sam Brown, wanted to have a private talk with him. Edward went to Sam's office. Sam asked Edward about the charges for arresting the two men. In desperation, Edward answered that the two men were arrested for suspicion of drug trafficking. Sam wanted Edward to submit a report. Edward told Sam that the report would be ready by late afternoon.

Edward decided to interrogate Rudy Bicciato first. Before that, Edward asked his colleagues about the result of their check on the car driven by Rudy Bicciato and Jack Smith. Edward's colleagues reported that the car was stolen. This was good news to Edward because it supported his case for arresting the two men. Edward reasoned that both Rudy and Jack were tailing him because of his investigation on his sister's death. To Edward, the single common link between the CIA and the Mafia, was operation Bay of Pigs. Presently, he had to justify the arrests based on suspicion of drug trafficking. Hence, Edward pressured Rudy into confessing his involvement in drug trafficking. To Edward's surprise, Rudy admitted that he and Jack were involved in drug trafficking. This made it easy for Edward to justify the arrests. However, Edward thought that Rudy confessed in order to avoid something more important, from being uncovered. In any case, Edward still wanted more information on what led to his sister's death. Thus, Edward questioned Jack.

Edward made sure that Jack was isolated from Rudy. When Edward and Jack were alone in the interrogation room. Edward said, "Rudy told me all about Del Charro Hotel and the Bohemian Grove." Jack gasped and exclaimed, "So you know all about PERMINDEX!" Edward was surprised, but he did not show it. Jack suddenly realized that he might have volunteered more information and clamped up. Edward questioned further, but Jack was silent. Instead, he demanded his right to call up his lawyer.

When Edward was preparing his report, he was summoned to Sam's office. Sam instructed Edward to release both men. Edward asked Sam for his reasons, but Sam told Edward that it was based on a need to know basis. Edward was frustrated, but he realized that Sam's reaction was the result of intervention by higher authorities.

Edward gave the order to release both men. Jack sneered at Edward, "We'll meet again." Edward responded, "Next time, you won't be so lucky."

Edward sneaked out of the police station's side entrance; and drove his car across the street. He watched and waited, as the two men left the main entrance of the building. The two men hailed a taxi; and Edward tailed the two men to Hotel Trinity at Fort Worth. The two men went into the hotel, but Edward continued to wait outside. It was night when the two men left the hotel. The two men hailed another taxi and went to the Carousel Club near North Collett Avenue, Dallas, Texas. It was 1.00am when Edward saw the two men stagger out of the pub. They were heading towards Sycamore Street when a passing car fired machine guns at them. Then, the car sped off so fast that Edward was unable to give chase.

Edward drove his car near the two men. He could tell that Rudy was dead, but Jack groaned in pain. Edward got off his car and examined Jack's wound. A shot went clean through the rib cage on Jack's left side. Edward folded some rags in his car's boot and used them as bandage for Jack. Edward left Ruby where he laid while he took Jack to the nearest hospital. A doctor at the hospital cleaned the wound and applied some stitches. An X-ray was taken of Jack's rib cage. Edward informed about his police officer identity, to the hospital. The hospital reluctantly discharged Jack, after Edward claimed that Jack was an important eye witness and needed to be moved to a 'safe' house.

Edward booked Jack into a remote motel for the night. Edward helped Jack into a room and asked Jack about Permindex. This time Jack was more cooperative. Jack told Edward that the name PERMINDEX was a contraction for "Permanent Industrial Exhibition." It was set up in 1958, with Canadian lawyer Louis

Mortimer Bloomfield as its president and chairman of its board. Louis was a key figure in the Israeli lobby and an operative of the Canadian Jewish Bronfman family. After the Office of Strategic Services (OSS) was established in 1942, Louis was recruited and given the rank of major. In 1947, the OSS was closed down and replaced by the CIA (Central Intelligence Agency) which was created by British intelligence. Louis then did contract work for the CIA.

The main shareholder in Permindex was Geneva's Banque De Credit International, a bank founded by Tibor Rosenbaum. This bank was a Mossad front while Tibor Rosenbaum was a Mossad agent. The CIA, Mossad and many other intelligence agencies in the world were controlled by British intelligence MI-5 and MI-6, in a vast web of intrigue that had its global power base in the square mile City of London. The Mossad had close connections to Meyer Lansky's crime syndicate and the CIA, through James Angleton who operated COINTELPRO, the black ops division of the CIA. To date, the CIA was still loyal to the international bankers based in the City of London and the global elite aristocratic families such as the Windsor's and the Rothschild's. The banking houses of J. P. Morgan Company, Brown Brothers Harriman, Warburg, Kuhn Loeb and J. Henry Schroder firmly controlled the ten largest bank holding companies in the US. All of these banking houses have branches in London and all of them maintain close relationships with the House of Rothschild. Thus, the CIA had a London Connection; and it was the City of London with its associated global organizations.

Permindex was financed by oil companies and oilfield services company Halliburton. Two rich Texas oilmen, Clint Murchison and Sid Richardson, owned the Del Charro Hotel which provided pro bono entertainment and rooms to rich oilmen, politicians, military leaders and top government officials. Many guests of Del Charro Hotel were also club members of the secret Bohemian Grove. In the ranks of PERMINDEX were Nazis and neo-Nazis, terrorists and Mafia operatives. Hence, some guests of Del Charro Hotel were also members of PERMINDEX.

After Jack's briefing, Edward allowed Jack to sleep for an hour. Edward then woke up Jack and arranged for him to travel by coach to the town of Del Rio, near the Mexican border.

Edward knew that he was up against a formidable group of people, but he could not let his sister's murderers go free.

Trojan Horse Of The Banksters

Saturday morning 13 September 1963, someone lodged a police report of a homicide committed near Sycamore Street.

Edward drove to the scene of the crime with some of his colleagues. Edward and his team started the long process of taking photos at the crime scene, collecting clues and asking around for eye witnesses. It was a long day.

There were no leads at all, except that Rudy Bicciato was arrested on the night of 11 September 1963 on suspicion of drug trafficking. Edward prepared a report that Rudy was killed by a rival gang. Bullet casings found at the scene of crime, were evidence of a shootout.

Edward knew that he had to be careful because rich oilmen, politicians, military leaders, top government officials and the Mafia mob were involved. Edward concluded that he needed to obtain more information on operation Bay of Pigs.

Edward made a hasty dinner appointment with Miriam Zadok on Sunday night. Miriam readily agreed. During dinner, Edward told Miriam that he had information that another operation related to operation Bay of Pigs would be taking place. He informed Miriam that there were already some activities taking place between the CIA and the Mafia. Miriam was interested.

Edward asked Miriam to provide him with more details of operation Bay of Pigs. Miriam told him that during operation Bay of

Pigs, there was absence of any preparations for an organized uprising in Cuba. This led President Kennedy (JFK) to conclude that the Joint Chiefs of Staff and the CIA had assumed all along that he would drop restriction against the use of US forces; and send the Marines and the Navy jets into the action. However, JFK made up his mind not to involve any American combat troops or planes in this fight between the two Cuban political factions; even though the rebels had his approval and the support of the CIA. When reports of failure came from the beachhead, JFK refused to give in to his military advisers, he preferred the embarrassment of defeat than the use of American military force against a small nation.

That sad night at the White House, when JFK heard news of the defeat and capture of the Cuban rebels at the Bay of Pigs, he said to the generals and admirals, "I'll take the defeat and I'll take all of the blame for it." At the press conference that followed, the President made his remark about second-guessing on the Bay of Pigs disaster, "There's an old saying that victory had a hundred fathers and defeat is an orphan." The Bay of Pigs experience brought much significant changes in the Kennedy administration. The operations and authority of the CIA were being limited and tightened. Allen Dulles was forced to retire with JFK's good wishes; and was replaced by John McCone, a former chairman of the Atomic Energy Commission.

Edward thought that the Kennedy administration's limitation of CIA operation and authority would lead to restrictions in other related organizations. Edward wondered if JFK had known about the CIA link with the international bankers based in the City of London. Thus, Edward asked Miriam if JFK had taken any action against the international bankers. Miriam was surprised that a police officer was able to make such quick deductions.

Miriam informed Edward that on 4 June 1963, President John F. Kennedy signed Executive Order No. 11110 that returned to the US government the power to issue currency, without going through the Federal Reserve. JFK's order gave the Treasury the power "to issue silver certificates against any silver bullion, silver or standard silver dollars in the Treasury." With the stroke of a pen, JFK was on his way to putting the Federal Reserve Bank of New York out of business.

Edward asked Miriam about the relationship between the international bankers and the Federal Reserve. Miriam explained that the Federal Reserve was a private corporation set up by the international bankers. On the night of 22 November 1910, a delegation of leading financiers left the railway station at Hoboken, New Jersey, on a secret mission. The delegation was led by Senator Nelson Aldrich, head of the National Monetary Commission. The rest of the delegation were Assistant Secretary of the US Treasury Department, A. Piatt Andrew, Frank Vanderlip, Henry P. Davison, Charles D. Norton, Benjamin Strong, and Paul Warburg. These men met secretly on Jekyll Island, off the coast of the state of Georgia, to create the Federal Reserve System with its twelve equally autonomous "regional" banks. This 1910 plot to seize control of the money and credit of the US people, was planned by men who already controlled much US resources. Furthermore, they were themselves answerable to the foreign financial power of England, centered in the London Branch of the House of Rothschild. In 1913, the Federal Reserve Act became law.

The Federal Reserve Bank of New York was free to set monetary policy for the entire United States. The majority stock of the Federal Reserve Bank of New York was purchased by three New York City banks: First National Bank, National City Bank and the National Bank of Commerce. The principal stockholders of these banks showed a direct London connection. Thus, London became the world's financial center, as enormous sums of capital could be created at its command, by the US Federal Reserve Board. This then was a Trojan horse set up by the banksters with Rothschild at their helm.

Edward realized that JFK was on a collision course with the US Military, the CIA and the London connection. As he was immersed in his thoughts, Miriam asked Edward about the activities that took place between the CIA and the Mafia. Edward informed Miriam about the arrests of a CIA agent and a mobster. Edward also told Miriam about the death of the mobster, Rudy.

Miriam wanted to know about the details of another operation related to operation Bay of Pigs. Edward said that he overheard someone mentioned operation 'Bay of Pigs redacted' when he was in Las Vegas. Miriam reasoned that a repeat invasion of Cuba would not be envisaged by JFK. Furthermore, JFK could not be expected to fully cooperate with the CIA, much less the Mafia. Therefore, an operation resulting from operation Bay of Pigs would be a combined effort by the London connection, members of the US military, elements of the CIA and the Mafia.

Edward was more interested to focus on bringing his sister's murderers to justice. At the same time, Edward knew that he alone had no power or resources to deal with an operation of the same scale as operation Bay of Pigs. Edward thanked Miriam for her information; and they parted company after dinner.

When Edward reached home, he made up his mind to focus only on finding his sister's killers. However, he wondered on how operation Bay of Pigs was related to Bohemian Grove. Edward started to write notes on all that he had learnt in the last three days. Edward also drew a new chart on which he included PERMINDEX and linked it to the Mossad, Del Charro Hotel and the Bohemian Grove. Edward also linked the Mossad to the CIA which he then linked to the London connection.

Edward sat and thought about the next practical step. He decided to check on Clint Murchison who was the Texas oilman that owned Del Charro Hotel.

3

Operation Prometheus

G reek gods were symbolic of the ruling class. Prometheus was a member of the ruling families, but he betrayed his own kin by showing too much empathy for his people. In Greek mythology Prometheus was credited with the creation of man from clay and the theft of fire for human use, an act that enabled progress and civilization. He was known for his intelligence; and as a champion of mankind. Hence, to the Illuminati, Prometheus was a villain who deserved to be punished.

On 27 April 1961, JFK made a public speech about the power of secret societies and their worldwide conspiracy threatening the American people. To the Bolsheviks, this was a declaration of war by one man against the entire principalities and power in high places.

Camelot

Despite his youth, 43-year-old John Fitzgerald Kennedy captured the Democratic nomination in 1960. On 8 November 1960, JFK was elected president in one of the closest elections in US history. Kennedy was the youngest man ever elected president, the only Catholic, and the first president born in the twentieth century.

JFK's election win had the blessing and help of Illuminati member and Satanist, Aristotle Onassis. In September 1957, Aristotle met fellow Satanist, Joseph Kennedy (JFK's father); and it was decided to use the Mafia's power in getting John F. Kennedy elected.

JFK proved to be a worthy king of Camelot, to the frustration and disgust of the Illuminati elites. However, the knights of the Round Table were evil and only obeyed instructions from the City of London. These knights also belonged to an exclusive organization called the CFR (Council on Foreign Relations) founded in 1921, mainly through the "mysterious" Round Table "Insider" Col. Mandel House. The CFR was a front for the Jewish J. P. Morgan and Company; and was part of an international Anglophile (Anglo-Zionist) network. From the beginning, the king of Camelot could only depend upon his brother, US Attorney General, Robert Kennedy. Vice President Lyndon 'Lying' Johnson (LBJ) was unreliable since he was placed there by J. Edgar Hoover who blackmailed JFK, to get LBJ the post.

Lee Harvey Oswald The Saga

Lee Harvey Oswald was an American Secret Agent who was sent to Russia, posing as a defector. On 15 October 1959, Oswald left Helsinki by train which crossed the border into Russia at Vainikkala; and arrived in Moscow on 16 October 1959.

On June 1962, Attorney General Robert Kennedy arranged for Lee Harvey Oswald's return to the US from USSR. Oswald's new assignments were to spy on La Cosa Nostra leader, Carlos Marcello; and the CIA, for the US Kennedy Administration.

In April 1963, Oswald was allocated by the CIA, to be the bodyguard of Judyth Vary Baker who was doing a cancer research project led by Dr. Mary Sherman; and funded by right wing politicians and Texan oil barons. This cancer research initially started with the development of the polio vaccine which was created off monkey kidney cells. Later, it was discovered that the polio vaccine was contaminated with monkey viruses which caused cancer. This led to the secret experiments on cancer viruses in the town of New Orleans. The US military found that these cancer viruses such as the

SV 40 that was in the polio vaccine became Super Aggressive, once they were bombarded with various forms of radiation.

A related biological cancer virus weapon program was undertaken. Judyth Vary Baker and Lee Harvey Oswald stood side-by-side in an underground medical laboratory located in David Ferrie's apartment on Louisiana Avenue Parkway in New Orleans. Judyth was the laboratory technician that handled the cancer-causing monkey viruses which were being used to develop a biological weapon.

After the Bolsheviks learnt that Oswald was a secret agent for the Kennedy Administration, they decided to use him as a patsy in JFK's assassination. William Seymour and his gang of killers were instructed to kill Oswald after JFK was assassinated. Jack Ruby would be the backup to kill Oswald, in case the attempt failed. This would prevent information about the military industrial and pharmacological complex link to the current worldwide cancer epidemic, from being leaked out.

Bewitching Hour

Edward was totally immersed in his police work for a whole week. Most days he was too exhausted to look into his sister's case.

It was Sunday 22 September 1963, Edward took a short walk in the park. Then, he sat awhile on a park bench. Very soon Edward dozed off. Suddenly, Edward woke up to the sound of a pigeon flying over his head. He shifted on the park bench and gazed at the pigeon landing at a spot on the grass. The moment that he shifted, a bullet zipped past his right ear. Edward ducked onto the ground.

The park was strangely silent. Edward knew that he must find cover quickly. He dashed towards some trees, all the while he kept low. As he hid behind the trees, he looked around. There were no more shots. Edward looked at the park bench where he was sitting. The shot could either come from in front of him or behind him.

Edward took out his revolver and circled to an area in front of where he was sitting because that was where most of the bushes and trees were.

Satisfied that no one was around, Edward decided to leave the park quickly. On his way home, Edward thought about the assassination attempt on him. His mind took him to the events that involved Rudy and Jack. There was also an attempt to silence them. In addition, higher authorities had dictated the release of these two men, many hours before they were ambushed near the Carousel Club. Edward was suspicious that the two men were at the Club for another reason, than just having some drinks.

Back home, Edward pondered about the assassination attempt on his life. He must be getting too close in his investigation about his sister's death. He also wondered whether any of his colleagues were working undercover for some higher authorities. Perhaps operation Bay of Pigs Redacted was just a coded term for an operation resulting from the failure of operation Bay of Pigs.

Edward had a hunch that something big was about to happen. This event had the combined effort of the London connection, Texas oilmen, the US military, elements of the CIA and the Mafia. He prepared a new chart and wrote the words 'Big operation.' Then, he linked the London connection, Big Oil, US military, CIA and Mafia to 'Big operation.'

It was midnight when Edward retired to bed. Edward did not fall off to sleep immediately. His mind was flooded by random thoughts. Suddenly, Edward was aware of a presence in his room. A mist filled his room and Edward felt cold. Out of the mist, Edward saw Doris in a scarlet dress.

Edward sat up in bed and reached for his revolver. Then, Doris spoke to Edward in his mind. It was not an audible sound, but in his mind, Edward could hear Doris. "Do not be afraid," said Doris. "I mean no harm," she added. Doris said, "I heard that Jane died from my cousin Joseph, but I had nothing to do with it."

Edward was surprised because he could also converse with Doris in his thoughts. Edward asked "What happened?" "Your sister went to San Francisco with people she befriended earlier at Del Charro Hotel," answered Doris. "Were you the one who took Jane to Del Charro Hotel in January?" asked Edward. Doris exclaimed, "So you knew!"

"I was invited by a member of the Vlad Dracula family," answered Doris, "So I took Jane along for a good holiday at Del Charro Hotel."

"Whom did Jane met at Del Charro Hotel?" asked Edward.

Doris answered, "Distant relatives of the Vlad Dracula family." Doris added, "Oilman, George Herbert Walker Bush and his wife Barbara (Pierce) Bush were members of the Vlad Dracula family."

Just then, the mist and Doris vanished. Edward heard a flutter of wings outside the open window and a light breeze blew into the room.

The next morning, Edward woke up with the haunting memory of his meeting with Doris, still fresh in his mind.

Gunfight At Noon

Edward did some monotonous desk job at the police station. Just a few minutes before noon, Edward went to a nearby café with his colleague, Steve Dalton. Just as they crossed the road, a shot rang out; and a bullet struck the windscreen of a nearby car. Both Edward and Steve drew their pistols and ran for cover behind the same car.

Suddenly, a black car sped by with machine guns blazing at Edward and Steve. Police from across the road joined in the gunfight and fired at the black car. The driver of the black car was hit; and the car rammed against a lamppost. Two occupants from the black car jumped out and emptied their machine guns at the police. Meanwhile, Edward and Steve stood up and fired at the two men. One man fell to the ground dead and the other man surrendered.

The only man alive, was identified as William Bright from the FBI division 5. The dead driver was identified as Tim Agnew (aka Crocodile Joe), a mobster. The dead man with the machine gun was identified as Sam Conners from the CIA.

To Edward, three men from different organizations and working together, was confirmation of 'Big operation.' Edward reported the arrest to Sam Brown who gave Edward permission to interrogate William Bright.

Edward wanted to shock William Bright. Edward asked William, "Were you at the Carousel Club last night." Edward could tell that William was uneasy. There was a moment of silence, William hesitantly answered, "Just a couple of drinks."

"Whom did you talk to?" asked Edward. William sat up as though a bolt of lightning just passed through him. However, William did not answer.

Edward put on the pressure and said, "Of course you knew Jack Smith; you were together in the same operation." William nodded.

"What is the codename of this operation?" asked Edward. William answered in an almost inaudible voice, "The big event." Now was the time for Edward to be shocked—the name which he had labeled the operation was almost the same!

Edward asked "Who was Jack's direct supervisor?" William motioned Edward who came closer, then William whispered, "Bill Harvey."

Edward said, "We'll talk again tomorrow." William's face showed fear as he said, "Please release me." Edward assured him, "No one is going to hurt you here."

As Edward left William, he felt that William faced uncertain danger. Edward approached Sam for William's release. Sam said that shooting at the police was a serious crime. Edward suggested that William could be tailed so that the police would be able to find out the mastermind of the whole plot. Sam agreed. Edward arranged for William's release and prepared for police officers to tail William round the clock.

Since his release, William was tailed round the clock. He went to the Carousel club quite frequently; and was seen in the company of the club owner, Jack Ruby. Sometimes, William also took flights from Dallas-Fort Worth to New Orleans and met with Lee Harvey Oswald, Guy Banister and David Ferrie, at a local pub in Clinton, Louisiana.

The Calm Before The Storm

On 1 October 1963, Edward picked up William and brought him to the Dallas police Department for questioning.

Edward asked William about his meetings with Jack Ruby, Oswald (LHO), Guy Banister and David Ferrie. Immediately, William knew that he was being followed. William did not answer the first question.

Edward disclosed to William, what the police knew about Jack Ruby. Edward said, "We are aware that Jack Ruby's Carousel club is funded by Carlos Marcello who is the Mafia boss of New Orleans." William answered, "It is FBI business to monitor Mafia activities." Smiling, Edward asked, "Why are you monitoring a communist sympathizer like LHO. What has it to do with Mafia activities?"

William sat up with a stunned look. Edward continued with his questioning, "Are your recent activities, anything to do with the big event?" Reluctantly, William nodded.

Edward said, "I don't have the authority to help you out, but I have a reason to find out about the big event." William asked in a low voice, "Can you release me again so that we can talk?"

Edward nodded and made arrangements to free William while activating police officers to tail William again. Edward then sneaked out the side entrance to follow William.

Edward saw William heading towards the direction of the Carousel club. Edward got into his car and drove to Sycamore Street. Edward parked his car and waited in the vicinity of the Carousel club. Several minutes later, Edward saw William walking towards the Carousel club. Behind William was a police officer following in a distance. Edward briefly showed his face round the corner of a side lane. William noticed and followed Edward into the side lane. Edward dashed towards his car at Sycamore Street, with William following close behind.

Edward drove William to a secluded motel; and booked into a room. As soon as the door was locked, William told Edward that the big event was a plot to assassinate President Kennedy. Edward immediately knew that several groups would be involved. Edward asked about the date of the assassination. William told Edward that the assassination would be done in Texas.

Edward immediately knew that this job by PERMINDEX would be a massive operation, involving Texas Governor Connally. Edward said to William, "You are on your own now. I will drop you at San Antonio." As Edward was driving to San Antonio, William warned Edward that he was instructed to silence him by Cord Meyer who was the ultimate leader of Bill Harvey. William also informed Edward that some of the police at the Dallas Police Department was taking direct instructions from Governor Conally.

After Edward dropped William at San Antonio, he decided to contact Miriam. Miriam invited Edward for dinner at her home.

Edward did not return to his office. Instead, he picked up Miriam at the Texas Observer. Miriam then directed Edward to her home.

On the way to Miriam's home, Edward told her that there were two attempts on his life. Miriam told Edward to be careful.

At Miriam's home, she prepared a delicious dinner for Edward. Later, as they were drinking coffee, Edward informed Miriam that the event which resulted from the failed Bay of Pigs invasion was codenamed 'the big event.'

Edward told Miriam that the plot would involve Governor Conally of Texas and that there would be an assassination attempt on President Kennedy in Texas. In September 1963, the Kennedy tour through Texas (including Dallas) had already been announced in Dallas papers.

Miriam opened her mouth wide and stared in disbelief.

There were some minutes of silence, then Miriam spoke, "What can we do?" Edward said, "Nothing! We are up against a formidable force. No one around us can be trusted."

Miriam sighed.

Edward changed the subject and talked about Doris's visitation. Edward told Miriam that according to Doris, his sister's death had something to do with members of the Vlad Dracula family.

Miriam was amazed. She told Edward that the occult was pure evil; and she knew that Doris's family had their occult tradition for centuries.

As it was late in the evening, Edward thanked Miriam for the wonderful meal and her good company. He then left Miriam's house and drove off.

Along the way, Edward had a hunch that something would happen to him. Edward parked his car at another lane near his home. Edward stealthily darted among the bushes. In one of the houses, Edward could hear the chime of midnight by a wall clock.

4

The Fall Of Camelot

As Edward neared his home, he saw two figures in black clothing moving furtively towards the front door. Edward hid behind a nearby tree.

Suddenly behind him, Edward felt someone closing in on him. Edward looked behind and saw another figure in black clothing who pointed a gun at him. Just then, Edward saw Joseph Baren moved behind this stranger and broke his neck like a twig.

The other two strangers heard the commotion and looked towards Joseph's direction. As they lifted their guns to fire at Joseph, he vanished from sight. In a flash, Joseph was behind one of the strangers. Grasping the stranger by the throat, Joseph bit his neck. The other stranger looked at Joseph's bloodshot eyes and froze in terror. Joseph moved towards the remaining stranger; and with his bare hands, he crushed the skull of the stranger.

Edward spoke with his mind, "This is horrible. It is not necessary." Joseph answered with his mind, "You better go now. I'll take care of the rest."

The Framing Of Lee Harvey Oswald

Edward drove in a daze and booked into a motel to stay for the night.

Next morning, Edward reported late for work. Edward saw a note on his desk about the disappearance of William. Edward instructed the police officers who were assigned the duty of tailing William, to submit him a report. The report was later forwarded by Edward to Sam Brown.

Late in the afternoon, Edward went with his colleague, Steve Dalton, to check on a homicide. As usual, clues were collected at the scene of the crime; and potential witnesses were identified. After their routine work, Edward and Steve walked towards their car. Suddenly, Steve pushed Edward to the ground and pulled out his pistol. Steve fired two shots at targets behind Edward. A bullet hit Steve on his hip and he crumbled to the ground. Edward looked behind him and saw two dead policemen. Edward ran to Steve who was groaning in pain. "Did you shoot the two policemen?" asked Edward. Steve replied, "They were going to shoot you."

Edward knew that there would be more attempts on his life. He had to find out the identity of the people who wanted him dead.

After the shooting incidence between Steve and the two police officers, there was an in-house investigation. However, a decision was suddenly made, to cease the investigation. Edward immediately knew that the higher authorities wanted to cover-up the shooting incidence.

Sam assigned Edward to check on the activities of a Lee Harvey Oswald who had just returned from New Orleans, in early October. L. H. Oswald was suspected of being associated with Jack Ruby and David Ferrie. Both Jack and David were known to be involved in drugs and weapons smuggling with some Cuban gangsters. There were also reports that Oswald had contacted David Ferrie in New Orleans.

Edward learned that since 24 April 1963, Oswald's wife and daughter had been staying in the home of Ruth Paine. Edward concluded that Oswald had special relations with Ruth Paine.

After several days of investigations on Ruth Paine, Edward concluded that Ruth Paine was probably an undercover CIA agent. In fact, Ruth Paine was introduced to Oswald and his wife in April 1963, by George de Mohrenschildt. Way back in 1952, Mohrenschildt worked for the oil millionaire, Clint Murchison. George de Mohrenschildt was an active member of the Dallas Council On World Affairs and the Crusade For A Free Europe; both of which were CIA organizations. Files of the CIA Office of Security reflect that Ruth Paine is the daughter of William Avery Hyde.

On 15 October 1963, Ruth Paine assisted Oswald in obtaining a job interview at the Texas School Book Depository. Oswald's first day of work at the Texas School Book Depository was on 16 October 1963. Edward discovered that Ruth Paine planted Oswald at the Texas School Book Depository, on 18 October 1963. Edward suspected that the CIA undercover agent, Ruth Paine, was positioning a member of the Mob, L. H. Oswald, as a sniper, in preparation of President Kennedy's ambush in Dallas.

Edward was low in spirit because he knew in advance that there would be an attempt on President Kennedy's life, but had no idea on what to do. Edward made a dinner appointment with Miriam.

During dinner Edward told Miriam about the plan for the gangster, Oswald, to be a sniper at the Texas School Book Depository. Edward informed Miriam that Oswald was associated with both Jack Ruby and David Ferrie who were known thugs.

Miriam volunteered to check on Jack Ruby and David Ferrie. They agreed to meet again in the following week, on 22 October 1963. On 22 October 1963, Edward picked up Miriam from her place of work at 6.30pm. They had an Italian dinner at the Sorrento Ristorante located in 415 Westheimer, Houston. It was a very cozy restaurant and both of them enjoyed each other's company. Over a glass of red wine, Miriam informed Edward that Jack Ruby, David Ferrie and L. H. Oswald, worked together for Guy Banister. Guy

Banister worked previously for the FBI and later, the New Orleans Police Department. After his dismissal from the Police Department, he operated his own private detective agency at 531 Lafayette Street, New Orleans. In 1963, Banister and David Ferrie began working for the lawyer G. Wray Gill and his client, Carlos Marcello. Marcello was the undisputed leader of the Mafia in New Orleans. JFK's brother, Attorney General Robert Kennedy, took steps to deport Marcello to Guatemala (the country Marcello falsely listed as his birthplace).

Miriam told Edward that recently, Jack Ruby had meetings with senior Mafia members such as Carlos Marcello and Santo Trafficante. Also, Oswald was seen visiting Jack Ruby at the Carousel club. According to Miriam, since the beginning of 1963, Carlos Marcello and Santo Trafficante had made plans with Jimmy Hoffa, to kill JFK. Hoffa was the president of the Teamsters Union; and had been investigated by Robert Kennedy for corruption. Therefore, it would not be a surprise for Jimmy Hoffa wanting to kill both JFK and Robert Kennedy.

Edward was impressed by Miriam's information. He told Miriam that there appeared to be a network of people from the Mafia, CIA and FBI, all wanting to assassinate President Kennedy. In particular, he was assigned to investigate on Oswald on drug and weapons trade. Hence, he intended to visit Oswald with all the information which he had now uncovered.

Meeting With Oswald

Edward decided to meet with Oswald. On the morning of 23 October 1963, Edward went to the Texas School Book Depository 411 Elm Street, Dallas; and looked for Oswald. Edward did not wear his police uniform, nor did he reveal himself as a representative of the Dallas Police Department.

The staff directed Edward to the second floor lunchroom. About five minutes later, Oswald joined Edward in the lunchroom.

Edward introduced himself to Oswald, as Sergeant Edward Field from the Dallas Police Department. Edward noticed that Oswald sat up stiff as soon as he heard that Edward was a police officer. Edward asked Oswald on his associations with Jack Ruby and David Ferrie. Oswald answered with pursed lips, "We worked together at a private Detective Agency in New Orleans."

Edward asked, "Are you still in contact with Jack?" Oswald glanced at Edward and blinked his eyes. Oswald answered in a cautious tone, "I need to talk to my lawyer."

Edward said, "This is just a casual meeting. I have no intention of arresting you, but I am aware of the big event." Oswald did not show any emotions. Edward continued, "My superior wanted me to check whether you were engaged with Jack and David in criminal activities. I have just stumbled on the plan of the big event."

Oswald gave a measured response, "I am not in league with Jack and David. What are you going to do about the big event?" Edward answered, "Nothing that I can do about it, I can't even trust my own colleagues." Oswald nodded.

Oswald said, "I am working for the authorities. For this reason, my wife and daughter are staying with Ruth Paine while I lived alone elsewhere. Ruth Paine got me the job here, but I know that she is an undercover CIA agent." Edward asked, "Why are you allowing your wife and daughter to stay with someone who might be involved in the big event?"

Oswald gave a wry grin and asked, "Wouldn't that be the safest place for my loved ones? Why would I be working here, as arranged by Ruth Paine?" Suddenly, it dawned on Edward that Oswald was working on a dangerous assignment for the US government.

Edward asked, "Do you know what Jack and David are up to?" Oswald answered, "They are cooperating with Carlos Marcello and Santo Trafficante, in the big event."

Edward shook hands with Oswald. As Edward was walking away, Oswald said, "Governor John Connally is involved in the big event."

Edward pondered about Oswald's last few words; and realized that Governor John Connally would be the ultimate mastermind behind the assassination attempts on him. In fact, Edward concluded that Connally would be equally involved in the assassination plot on President Kennedy.

As Edward left the Texas School Book Depository, he gave a visual survey of the area. There must be a reason for Ruth Paine to arrange for Oswald's work in the Texas School Book Depository, Edward thought. Then, he noticed the seven storey Dal-Tex Building at 501 Elm Street. It was just across the street from the Texas School Book Depository in Dealey Plaza. As Edward took a closer look at the Dal-Tex Building, he thought that this would be a perfect place to shoot at President Kennedy's motorcade. Especially when there was an external fire escape staircase leading all the way to the rooftop.

On 28 October 1963, Edward looked up his colleague, Steve, still convalescing at the hospital. Doctors removed a bullet from Steve's hip and inserted two stainless steel pins into the fractured hip bone. The recovery was slow and Steve had to move around in crutches.

Edward confided with Steve and told him about operation big event. Steve was shocked about the plot to assassinate President Kennedy. However, Steve agreed that they had to lie low because they were not in any position to blow the whistle.

After visiting Steve, Edward decided to thank Joseph for saving his life.

The next day, Edward drove to the Crescent Court Branch of the JP Morgan Chase Bank. Edward parked his car and walked into the JP Morgan Chase Bank. It did not take him long to find Joseph. Joseph took Edward to the same Café for a cup of coffee.

Edward thanked Joseph for saving his life. Joseph informed that he was requested by Doris to protect Edward. Joseph said, "You are a threat to the Vlad Dracula clan. Normally, we do not interfere with what other Satanist families are doing. However, members of the Vlad Dracula clan have stormed the Las Vegas mansion of my cousin, Doris, to look for you."

Edward was surprised and exclaimed, "I did not engage in any hostile act against the Vlad Dracula clan!" Joseph explained, "Our species can smell you a mile away. You know that we can also detect your thoughts. You smell almost like your sister Jane whom they have killed. Doris treats your sister as a personal friend and she thinks that she has to respond in kind. You are now under our protection."

Edward asked, "Do you know about operation big event?" Joseph answered, "Yes. The Vlad Dracula family is among those plotting against President Kennedy."

Edward requested for more information. Joseph said, "Several Satanist families have combined their resources and power, to take over the world. These families control much of the world's finance from the City of London. The monarchies of Europe are all related and is one huge Satanist family known as the 'Black Nobility'." Edward heard this for the first time and was deeply troubled.

Edward thought to himself about the present circumstances relating to operation big event. Joseph answered with his mind, "Since the time of US President Woodrow Wilson until now, Satanist families have controlled the USA. Suddenly, US President J. F. Kennedy is trying to return the control of the US back to its own people. Many Jews cannot allow the Goyims to call the shots.

Therefore, they are using their various networks to plan and execute operation big event." Edward immediately knew that President Kennedy would soon be dead.

The Murchison Party

On 21 November 1963, a party was held at Clinton Murchison's home in Dallas. The party was hosted in the late afternoon by Murchison's son, John, on behalf of his father who had a stroke. The party was attended by Dallas tycoons, FBI moguls and organized crime kingpins. Nearing the end of the party, Lyndon B. Johnson (LBJ) arrived. Tension immediately filled the room upon LBJ's arrival. The group consisting of Haroldson L. Hunt, J. Edgar Hoover, Clyde Tolson, Jack Ruby, John J. McCloy and Richard Nixon, immediately went behind closed doors, for a private meeting. After the meeting, LBJ reappeared. Squeezing the hand of his mistress, Madeleine Brown, LBJ spoke with a grating whisper into her ear, "After tomorrow those goddamn Kennedys will never embarrass me again—that's no threat—that's a promise."

Having finalized the plot to terminate President Kennedy, LBJ left for the Houston Coliseum to attend a dinner and speech by JFK. JFK and LBJ flew out around 10pm and arrived at Carswell (Air Force Base in northwest Fort Worth) at 11:07pm.

The Tragedy Of America

It was 22 November 1963, President Kennedy was to be transported in a motorcade procession from Love Field airport to the luncheon site of Trade Mart. Right from the start, secret service agents such as Emory P. Roberts, George Hickey, William Greer, Roy Kellerman and Winston G. Lawson were complicit in the plot to murder JFK. Indications, of Secret Service complicity in the assassination of John F. Kennedy, were the absence of protective military presence, lack of coverage of open windows, Secret Service agents failure to ride on the Presidential limousine, the improper arrangement of vehicles, the Secret Service driver braking the vehicle to a halt after gun shots were being fired, the lack of response by Secret Service agents, the driver washing the car's back seat at Parkland Hospital, the car being dismantled and rebuilt (on LBJ's orders), the replacement of windshields, the autopsy photos being taken into custody before they were developed.

After the motorcade passed the Texas School Book Depository, all hell broke loose. Edward was standing near the front entrance of the Texas School Book Depository, watching activities at the Dal-Tex Building. Edward saw flashes of at least two shots being fired from the rooftop of the Dal-Tex Building, but no shots were fired from the Texas School Book Depository.

After the shooting, five men hurriedly walked down the external fire escape staircase of the Dal-Tex Building. Edward decided to follow the fifth man who was running towards the Grassy Knoll. On top of the Grassy Knoll, Edward saw the man running towards a car park. Edward was about one hundred feet from the man who was about to enter a car at the car park. When Edward came into full view, the driver of the car shot the man and sped off. Edward went to examine the man and found that he had died.

After the assassination of JFK, J. Edgar Hoover and the Federal Bureau of Investigation helped to cover-up the real identity of the people who assassinated JFK.

"For we wrestle not against flesh and blood, but against principalities, powers, against the rulers of the darkness of this world, against spiritual wickedness in high places" (Ephesians 6:12)

At the gravesite of US President John F. Kennedy in Arlington National Cemetery, the eternal flame of Prometheus was lit. This flame symbolized that JFK who betrayed the globalist ruling class, was punished by the Illuminati. The Illuminati being the rulers of the darkness of this world, supported by satan and his demons, still reign supreme.

Eternal Flame Of Prometheus

When King Arthur was murdered by the treacherous knights of the Round Table, Camelot was no more. Only the Round Table remained.

After JFK died, the US continued to be ruled by the London Connection. In particular, some of those who had a hand in JFK's assassination, such as LBJ, Richard Nixon, Ronald Reagan, Gerald Ford and H. W. Bush, took turns to be the US President.

In his post of unelected US President, LBJ immediately established the Warren commission, to cover up all the crime trails and gave US citizens the official lie about JFK's assassination. This Endeavour was supported by J. Edgar Hoover who used the FBI to destroy evidences, threaten and/or murder witnesses and lock up or destroy revealing documents, photos and other objects.

5

Operation Cyanide And
Restoration Of Jerusalem

The Bolsheviks achieved a coup d'etat when Zionist Jew, Lyndon 'Lyin' Johnson (LBJ), became the unelected President of the United States. The US was now effectively under the control of the foreign power of Israel. The Zionists called the shots and could use all the resources of the US, economic and military, to achieve the goal of a New World Order under 'Greater Israel.'

To establish 'Greater Israel,' LBJ initiated **Operation Cyanide**; and to establish the New World Order, LBJ initiated **Operation Condition November**. Both schemes were classified and running simultaneously.

The Attack On USS Liberty

On 5 June 1967, Israel launched a preemptive strike against the neighboring states of Egypt (aka United Arab Republic (UAR)), Jordan and Syria. The war began with a large-scale air strike by Israel on Egypt. At the Security Council meeting of 5 June 1967, "Israeli officials, Eban and Evron, swore that Egypt had fired first." This was not the case, the US Office of Current Intelligence ". . . soon concluded that the Israelis—contrary to their claims—had fired first." Abba Eban, Israel's foreign minister during the war, later wrote in his autobiography that Nasser's assurances he wasn't planning to attack

Israel were credible: "Nasser did not want war. He wanted victory without war."

To LBJ, the preemptive strike by Israel on Egypt, Jordan and Syria, is the beginning of Operation Cyanide. Days before, the USS Liberty, an unarmed technical research ship used for intercepting electronic communications, was sent to collect electronic intelligence off the coast of the Sinai Peninsula. With the outbreak of war on 5 June 1967, Captain William L. McGonagle of the Liberty asked Vice Admiral William I. Martin at the US Sixth Fleet headquarters to send a destroyer as an armed escort of the Liberty. On June 6, Admiral Martin replied: "Liberty is a clearly marked United States ship in international waters, not a participant in the conflict and not a reasonable subject for attack by any nation."

In the morning of 8 June 1967, on 9 separate occasions Israeli planes flew out from the Sinai Peninsula to investigate the ship. At 2pm of 8 June 1967, the Israelis attack the USS Liberty with unmarked Mirage jets, launching rockets, strafing the ship with cannon fire. During the attack, the Liberty's five American radio channels were jammed. Israelis jets even shot at the officers and enlisted men stretched out on the deck for a lunch-hour sun bath. Eight crewmen were killed immediately. The Mirages left after expending their ammunition, and were replaced by two Dassault Mysteres armed with napalm bombs. The Mysteres dropped their payloads over the ship and strafed it with their cannons. Much of the ship's superstructure caught fire. At the time, the ship was in international waters north of the Sinai Peninsula, about 29.3 mi (47.2 km) northwest from the Egyptian city of Arish.

During the attack, antennas were severed, gas drums caught fire, and the ship's flag was knocked down. With a makeshift antenna, McGonagle sent an urgent request for help to the Sixth Fleet, "Under attack by unidentified jet aircraft, require immediate assistance." Eleven minutes later the USS Saratoga acknowledged receiving the message and Captain Joseph M. Tully ordered 12 F-4 jets and other refueling aircraft to go to the assistance of the Liberty and informed Sixth Fleet Commander Admiral William Martin. Within minutes after launch an order came down from the flagship, the USS Little Rock, to recall the planes. This was done on orders from Defense Secretary Robert McNamara. Sixth Fleet carrier division commander Lawrence Geis transmitted the message to the Saratoga to recall the planes, but he also told Captain Tully to prepare to launch planes 90 minutes later.

As part of Operation Condition November, the aircraft carrier USS America dispatched eight aircraft. These aircraft were armed with nuclear bombs when they took off. As arranged by LBJ, a nuclear strike had been ordered against Egypt. The US embassy in Cairo was notified that an attack was coming. This was another attempt to start a nuclear war with the Soviet Union! However, the USS Liberty was kept afloat by its crew who refused to die. Secretary of Defense, Robert McNamara from the Pentagon, immediately ordered the aircrafts recalled. Vice-Admiral William I. Martin obeyed the instruction minutes later. Thus, the plan to start a nuclear war with the Soviet Union had to be aborted again.

As a result of an earlier order by Commander Lawrence Geis, another group of planes took off at 3.45pm. At 4.39pm, McNamara ordered the recall of these planes. Commander Geis challenged McNamara's order about not launching any rescue aircraft; and President Johnson comes on the line. LBJ told the 6th Fleet commander that he "doesn't give a damn if the ship sinks. We're not going to embarrass an ally." The record about what McNamara and LBJ said were from an account by Liberty intelligence officer David Lewis who privately met with Geis after Liberty survivors were rescued.

While rescue planes were launched and then recalled, the USS Liberty came under attack by Israeli torpedo boats. The Liberty was hit by a torpedo on the starboard side, opening a large hole in the hull, and lists 10 degrees. More crew members died. The surviving sailors prepared to abandon ship. However, the torpedo boats machine gunned the life rafts. Israel's original intent was to leave no survivors so that a lie could be fabricated that Egypt had sunk a US ship, with all hands on deck! After more than two hours of unremitting assault, the Israelis finally halted their attack. Finally, 16 hours after the attack two US destroyers reached the Liberty. As the wounded were being evacuated, an officer with the Office of Naval Intelligence instructed the men not to talk about their ordeal with the press.

The following morning Israel launched a surprise invasion of Syria, breaching a new ceasefire agreement and seizing control of the Golan Heights.

Altogether, thirty-four men were killed in the attacks and over 170 wounded. Later, Israel explained that its air and naval forces had mistaken the Liberty for a much smaller Egyptian Navy ship, a 1920's era horse carrier. In a signed affidavit, retired Captain Ward Boston divulged that President Johnson and Defense Secretary McNamara ordered those heading the Navy's inquiry into the Liberty attack to conclude that the attack was a case of mistaken identity, despite overwhelming evidence to the contrary. In 1997, at Arlington National Cemetery, Captain of the USS Liberty, William McGonagle, stated publicly that the attack was intentional.

Blood Of A Babylonian Talmudic High Priest

The USS Liberty incidence occurred during the six days war (June 5 to 10, 1967) which was orchestrated by Israel. Due to the element of surprise in Israel's preemptive strike on Egypt, Jordan and Syria, Israel gained much territory. Israeli forces had taken control of the Gaza Strip and the Sinai Peninsula from Egypt, the West Bank and East Jerusalem from Jordan, and the Golan Heights from Syria.

The ploy of the Bolsheviks to provide a pretext for pre-emptive attacks by Zionist 'Israelis' on neighboring Arab nations, reached a milestone with the capture of Jerusalem. It was claimed that this was the fulfillment of "**the end of time of the Gentiles**." As the Ashkenazi Jews were 'Gentiles' who worshiped Satan in their Talmudic Judaism, Jerusalem was still being trampled underfoot by Gentiles. According to Ezekiel 38 and 39, the people from the north, in places such as Togarmah, Magog, Meshech and Tubal were all mentioned in the great end time invasion of the land of Israel. They were the INVADING army that God promised to bring against His land. Hence, Ezekiel prophesied the end-time invasion by the following nations:

1) Magog (Khazaria);
2) Turkey (Meshech [Mushki]; Tubal [Tabal], Gomer [Gimarrai], Togarmah [Tilgarimmu]);
3) Iran (Persia);
4) Ethiopia (Northern Sudan) and
5) Libya (Put)

A powerful demon called Gog, the Prince of Meshech and Tubal, was leading the attack upon Palestine. "Thus the Lord had shown me; and behold a swarm of locusts were coming, among the young devastating locusts was Gog, the king." (Amos 7:1) A similar mention of Gog was also found in the book of Revelation "And (the locusts) had a king over them, who is the angel of the bottomless pit. His name in Hebrew is Abaddon; but in Greek, his name is Apollyon." **(Rev. 9:11)**

The Jews were overjoyed that finally they had control of Jerusalem; and could pray at the 'wailing wall.' To them, it was Jehovah (aka Baal) of the Babylonian Talmud that had restored their nation of Israel. The Israelis now looked forward to the subjugation of every nation under Greater Israel.

It was more than three years since the murder of Edward's sister in 1963. Edward was not idle. Edward studied the Kabbalah. Edward also paid frequent visits to Clive Barker and Grant Thomson at the

University of North Texas, to discuss the Kabbalah and politics. Edward knew that the Jewish Globalists had regained control of the US; and US citizens were subjected to propaganda from the Jewish controlled media. Most of the US people were living in a world of Illuminati matrix built up by Hollywood, television and the press. President Kennedy's warning against secret societies were forgotten; and Edward knew that the worse was yet to come.

Over time, Edward built up a special relationship with Miriam. They had dinner together at least twice a week. Sometimes, Edward would go to Miriam's house in the night and talked about current world affairs. Recently, Miriam was briefing Edward on stories behind the six days war started by Israel. They also touched upon the topic of Israel's attack on the USS Liberty, but there were scant reports of this incidence. Thus, Edward had to rely on Miriam's information from other sources. Both Edward and Miriam concluded that the US government was in league with the London connection, for world conquest.

Occasionally, Doris or Joseph would visit Edward at his home, in the middle of the night. Due to such visits, Edward developed the ability to read the minds of other people. In particular, Edward identified corrupt police officers who were assisting the Mafia in various crimes.

It was 20 June 1967 that Edward applied for a ten days leave. Edward told Miriam that he would be away for ten days. Miriam did not ask any questions because she knew Edward well enough not to interfere too much in his personal life.

Edward's leave was approved the next day. Edward then booked an airline ticket for a trip to California, on the afternoon of 22 June 1967. In California, Edward checked into a hotel for the night. The next morning, Edward rented a car to drive to the 2,700-acre (1,100 ha) Bohemian Grove camp ground located at 20601 Bohemian Avenue, in Monte Rio, California. Along the way, Edward dropped off for lunch at Village Inn & Restaurant off River Boulevard, Monte Rio, California.

After lunch, Edward explored part of the Russian river from Monte Rio to Rio Nido. Rio Nido consists of summer homes, cabins, a few small businesses, a bar/restaurant, public pool and a small resort hotel. Edward decided to check into the local small resort hotel for the night.

Next day, Edward walked to the Russian river and asked several locals about directions to the Bohemian Grove. Finally, Edward met an elderly man who would be willing to lead Edward, part of the way. As they walked down a track together, Edward introduced himself to the elderly man. The elderly man introduced himself as Kelvin Summer. Edward asked Kelvin whether he could recall the discovery of a body near the Russian river, in 1963. Kelvin scratched his graying beard and said, "Things like that don't happen around these parts. In 1963, some hikers did discover body parts in some bushes at the Russian riverside near Monte Rio."

Edward and Kelvin continued walking towards the Bohemian Grove. Sometimes the track would be obstructed by broken branches, but they had no difficulty in climbing over the branches. As they neared the Bohemian Grove, Kelvin apologized and said, "This is where I've got to go. Have a nice day." With that Kelvin left Edward to explore on his own.

Soon, Edward reached some barbed wire fencing demarcating the boundary of the Bohemian property. Edward climbed over the fence and walked towards a giant Californian Redwood tree. Edward took out his penknife and carved a large "E" on the trunk of the tree, then he went back the previous route. Along the way, he would scratch marks on the trunk of trees so that he could find his way back again.

Edward returned to the small resort hotel at Rio Nido and stayed another night. Next morning, Edward went early to the Bohemian

Grove. He reached the previously marked giant redwood tree by 11.00am. Edward explored the grounds of the Bohemian Grove and found many camps. At a camp called 'Lost Boys,' Edward found a few friendly men who offered him food and drinks. Edward was happy to oblige. The men asked Edward whether he would join the annual gathering in Mid July. Edward nodded. Late in the afternoon, Edward left the camp and found his way into a gorge. He then hid among some trees to wait for nightfall.

Edward dozed off. Later, he was awaken just before dusk by the bizarre chanting and singing coming from the gorge. From behind a tree, Edward saw dozens of hooded men chanting and singing drunkenly beneath the giant redwoods. It was like the scene from a fairy tale. Huge skulls hung down from the floodlights, satanic-styled owls with glowing eyes, (trappings of death) that Edward saw in the twilight illuminated by the large floodlights. The revelers moved down paths towards a lake. Edward sneaked behind them from among trees and bushes. They went towards the northern tip of the lake, where a huge 40 feet stone owl and altar stood.

Edward joined the group and worked his way towards the front. Suddenly, a tall hooded man walked from behind the stone owl and stood at the altar. He saw Edward who was the only one without a hood; and pointed towards Edward. "Bring him to me!" he commanded.

Out of nowhere, a blood curdling scream was heard. Then, Doris in a scarlet dress leapt out from among the trees. Her hair was disheveled and her eyes were bloodshot. The group of hooded men backed away, as Doris glared at them. Then two of the men stepped out of the group and confronted Doris. Doris snarled as she leapt towards the two men; and tore off the right arm from one of them. Blood squirted out from the wound, as the injured man fell to the ground. Doris was in bare feet; and everyone saw that the feet was mutated and looked like the talons of an eagle. The group murmured; and someone blurted, "Lilith!"

The tall hooded man in front of the altar spoke, "You are interrupting our worship! I am a member of the Vlad Dracula clan." Doris answered, "You kidnapped and killed my friend. Today, I am making an example of you." Doris looked at Edward and said, "He is all yours."

The tall hooded man removed his hood and announced to Edward, "I am the high priest. You smell like someone that I have sacrificed. Her blood is very tasty." Edward saw that the high priest resembled Prince Charles of England, but he had cruel thin lips.

Edward spoke to the high priest with his mind, "Today! You will be reporting to Lucifer." The high priest was surprised that Edward had the ability to project his thoughts. Just then, Doris threw the severed arm at the high priest. In a flash, Edward took out his pistol and shot the high priest, in between the eyes. Edward looked around; and saw that the group had already fled. Doris told Edward to leave while she cleared up.

The Setting Sun

Two Days later, Edward and Miriam stood solemnly in front of Jane Field's grave. Then, Edward and Miriam were distracted by three people walking towards them. As the three people walked closer, Edward recognized that they were Doris, Joseph and Benjamin. Doris was holding a wooden box with both hands. She looked at Edward and said, "A dedication to your sister, Jane. This box contains the head of her killer." Miriam gasped and clung to Edward. Joseph produced a shovel and dug a hole below the tombstone of Jane. Doris carefully placed the wooden box into the hole. Joseph then shoveled some soil over the hole.

Edward introduced Joseph to Miriam. Joseph spoke to Miriam, "Doris and Benjamin told me all about you."

Doris took out a small flask from her handbag and unscrew the cap. She handed the flask to Edward and said, "This is the blood of the high priest." Edward took the flask and poured its contents over his sister's grave.

Doris said to Edward, "Now that you have closure, let us remain friends." Edward nodded and smiled. As dusk approached, a light breeze blew across the cemetery. A passing cloud threw its shadow across Doris, Joseph and Benjamin. After the cloud floated away, only Benjamin remained in front of Edward and Miriam. Joseph and Doris had vanished from the scene.

6

The Phoenix Assassination Program

Half past noon on the day of JFK's assassination, Dan Rather (from CBS News) was standing by the triple underpass south of Dealey Plaza waiting for a film drop from a camera crew that was following the presidential motorcade. They were late. Suddenly Dan saw the blur of the presidential limousine flash by and instinctively knew that something was wrong. Dan scrambled over an embankment; and saw the crowd of spectators from the Dealey Plaza, running in panic. Instead of making sense out of it, Dan ran back to the local CBS affiliate to break the story—whatever it was to the nation.

According to the Post, Johnson crouches in terror on the floor of his limousine, speeding to the relative safety of Dallas airport. Former CIA director Richard Helms casually admitted that he concealed crucial information about CIA's assassination plots against Castro from the Warren commission. Both Newsweek and the Post posited CIA fear of such a disclosure as being at the heart of the Warren commission's cover-up about JFK's assassination.

The same phantoms who lurked in the shadows of Dealey Plaza reappeared in Vietnam, where the CIA ran the Operation Phoenix assassination program. In the Golden Triangle area of Laos, Thailand and Cambodia, the CIA expedited the drug trafficking of its 'assets' in the alleged fight against communism. These expedited drugs were bound for American streets which brought in the 'pop' culture. In both Central America and Afghanistan, the recruitment of CIA assets and the expansion of the drug trade went hand in hand.

For nearly a century, the US had morphed to be a part of the British empire and evolved to be the leading country of the British empire. Hence, it acquired the characteristics of a Mafia type organization because that was the nature of the British empire. The primary and most important economic activity being the drug trade. As such, it would be natural for it to have policies relating to assassinations of its own leaders, critics and citizens. In addition, it also had policies relating to assassinations of major world leaders, such as Lumumba under Eisenhower, Castro and Diem under Kennedy, Gaddafi under Reagan, Saddam Hussein under Bush and Allende under Nixon. Of course, the US generated kill lists under direct presidential authority, for the targeted killing of thousands of civilians suspected of being or harboring alleged terrorists / insurgents, from Vietnam to Guatemala, from Indonesia to Iraq, and so on.

On 4 August 1964, United States President L. B. Johnson deceitfully claimed that North Vietnamese forces had twice attacked American destroyers in the Gulf of Tonkin. The Gulf of Tonkin was a body of water located off the coast of North Vietnam and South China. It was the northern arm of the South China Sea. Known today as the Gulf of Tonkin Incident, this event spawned the Gulf of Tonkin Resolution of 7 August 1964 that the US Congress passed. This gave President LBJ authorization, without a formal declaration of war by Congress, for use of "conventional" military force in Southeast Asia.

From 1965 to 1968, US and Saigon intelligence services maintained an active list of Vietcong cadres marked for assassination. In 1969, the Phoenix Program called for "neutralizing" 1,800 suspects each month. About one third of Vietcongs targeted for arrest had been summarily executed. Security committees were established in provincial interrogation centers, to determine the fate of Vietcong suspects, outside judicial controls. Green Berets and navy SEALs were most common recruits for the Phoenix Program. Green Beret detachment B-57 provided administration cover for other intelligence units. One was Project Cherry, tasked to assassinate Cambodian officials suspected of collaborating with the North Vietnamese and the KGB officials. Another was Project Oak targeted against South Vietnamese suspected collaborators. They controlled by special assistant for counterinsurgency and special activities, which worked with CIA outside of General Creighton Williams Abrams control.

Prelude To The Pegasus File

It was in early March 1968 that Edward proposed to Miriam, for her hand in marriage. Miriam gladly accepted Edward to be her lawfully wedded husband. Both Edward and Miriam decided to marry in mid April 1968. Edward renovated his house and went with Miriam to shop for furniture and other items, for their new home.

Edward and Miriam were not high income earners, so they planned their wedding expenditures within their means.

Their church wedding was attended by close friends and relatives. After their wedding, they went on a tour to Singapore and Thailand, during their honeymoon.

After touring Singapore for three days, Edward and Miriam flew to Bangkok. They checked into the Royal River Hotel located right on the western bank of Chao Phraya River. Edward had done some reading on Thailand; and he wanted to take Miriam on a river cruise the next day. In the night, they went to the busy Patpong night market situated in the built-up area known as Silom. The place was always busy and chaotic, with all the commotion from the Go-Go bars nearby. This market was Bangkok's notorious nightlife district. Miriam enjoyed the shopping and tried the exotic snacks.

The next day, Edward and Miriam took a cruise down the Chao Phraya River. There were also some canals on the Thon Buri side which is a pleasant way to explore parts of Bangkok city. In the evening, Edward and Miriam continued with a dinner cruise down the Chao Phraya River, aboard a cruiser. A wide selection of international and Thai delicacies were served, while they enjoyed delightful moments with the panoramic view of Bangkok at night. On board the cruiser, a music performance spiced up their cruise on the river. Sightseeing a night on Bangkok main river, gave them another vision of Thailand's capital, Bangkok.

Edward and Miriam then booked a domestic flight from Bangkok to Chiang Mai in northern Thailand. They checked into Palm Springs City Resort at 122 Moo 5, Mahidol Road, Chiang Mai. This hotel was just 15 minutes from the airport and the crowded city center, it enjoyed one of the finest garden locations in Chiang Mai. The eyes of Edward and Miriam, feasts on a tranquil landscape of rolling green lawns, lakes and swaying palms.

In the morning, Edward and Miriam took an early morning stroll to a nearby village. They walked into a village eating house, for a cup of coffee and some hard boiled eggs. Both felt relaxed and enjoyed each other's company.

All of a sudden, their world was shattered by the appearance of a group of men in tattered army fatigues. These men brandished submachine guns and were shouting in a local Thai dialect. The leader of the group was a Caucasian man with cold blue eyes and a permanent deep scar on his left cheek. He walked menacingly towards Edward and Miriam. "Take that woman," the leader commanded. Two men stepped forward and forcefully grasped Miriam's arms. Miriam resisted and Edward shouted to the leader, "Leave her alone!" Without a word, the leader thrust his rifle butt onto Edward's left temple. Edward dropped to the floor and his vision blurred. Miriam shouted for help. An elderly man ran out of the kitchen to investigate the commotion. The leader shot the man in the chest. The leader then pointed his gun at Edward. Just then, there were sounds of pistol shots. The leader and the group of men hastily abandoned the place, with Miriam as their prisoner.

By this time, Edward blacked out. When Edward regained consciousness, two police officers were by his side; and a woman was wiping his face with a damp cloth. Edward showed his police identification, from his wallet. One police officer said in perfect American accent, "I am officer Jack Bhumipol, trained by LAPD." "How long was I out?" asked Edward. Jack said, "About 15 minutes." "I've got to go after those thugs! They kidnapped my wife." exclaimed Edward. "We'll catch up with them. Let us show you the way." Jack assured Edward. "First let me request for backup." Jack told Edward. Then, Jack used the phone from the eating house to call his office.

Within a few minutes, Edward was in a police car with Jack and his assistant. Jack's assistant drove the police car at high speed on a road leading to Lampang town, in the valley of the Wang River in North Thailand. Jack explained to Edward that he suspected the group worked under the direction of a task force at Nakhon Phanom, Thailand. Within one hour they were in Lampang city. There they rested for five minutes; and they were off to Uttaradit Airport. Jack told Edward that the group would probably fly in a private plane.

On the way, Edward gave a description of the leader to Jack. Jack said, "He is probably a CIA paramilitary specialist." Edward asked, "What are they doing in your country?" Jack told Edward, "They are fighting a secret war across the border in Laos and Cambodia. My country allows them to operate from Nakhon Phanom." After about forty five minutes of driving from Lampang city, they reached the city of Phrae in the Phrae province.

Jack told Edward that they would be waiting for police reinforcements to arrive. As they were sitting in the police car, Edward heard Miriam's thoughts in his mind. In her thoughts, Miriam said to herself, "I hope Edward is not badly hurt by that brute!" Edward knew that Miriam must be nearby. Edward tried projecting his thoughts to Miriam, "Miriam! Can you hear me?" Edward heard Miriam's reply, "Is this real?" Edward responded, "This is for real. Can you describe your surrounding scenery?"

Edward heard Miriam's thoughts, "There are trees everywhere! I saw a waterfall nearby." Edward turned around and asked Jack, "Where is the waterfall?" Jack told Edward, "There is a 2-level Namtok Mae Khaem Waterfall at Tambon Suan Khuan. How do you know about any waterfall?" Edward said, "We need to get there, my wife is near that location. Sorry, I can't explain now!" Jack nodded and said, "My reinforcements are turning up anytime now. We'll head there soon."

Two jeeps of police reinforcements arrived in five minutes time. Jack directed them to rendezvous at the waterfall near Tambon Suan Khuan. In half an hour, the police force were assembled at the area. Edward projected his thoughts to Miriam, "We are near you."

Miriam replied, "I am in a bamboo cage enclosure with three other females. I can hear you much clearer now." Edward told Jack that his wife was imprisoned in a bamboo enclosure with three other females. Jack informed Edward that these people were engaged mainly in the drug trade, but occasionally they were also involved in sex slave trade.

The police fanned out and proceeded cautiously. In a jungle clearing, they asked directions from a local villager. The local villager directed them to a group of wooden huts with barbed wire fencing. The local villager told them that there were armed men staying in the wooden huts.

Jack arranged for the police to surround the huts. Edward and Jack approached the main gate which was guarded by two sentries. Jack identified himself as a police officer. The sentries told Jack that the area was a base camp for US operations; and no one could gain entry without any authorization from either the Thai government or the US government. Jack told the sentries that some of the men had committed crimes and demanded to see their superior. One of the sentries escorted Jack and Edward to see their superior. As Jack and Edward walked among the huts, Edward saw a large compound on his right.

Group Of Wooden Huts

Edward stepped towards the right and was immediately confronted by two men. One was a tall aggressive looking local while the other was the Caucasian with the cold blue eyes and a permanent deep scar on his left cheek. "So we meet again," sneered the Caucasian, as he reached for a gun at his right hip holster. Edward immediately rushed at the local and yanked a rifle from the local's hands. At that moment, the Caucasian swung around to face Edward. Without a thought, Edward swung the rifle butt at the Caucasian's right hand. The Caucasian dropped the gun and yelled in pain. Just then, the local man regained his balance; and taking a dagger, rushed at Edward. Edward reacted and fired the rifle at the face of the local man. Blood splattered on Edward, as the man crumpled to the ground.

In the din of the commotion, all hell broke loose. Shots rang out from everywhere. Edward saw that Jack was wounded in his left arm. Meanwhile, the Caucasian tried to retrieve his gun. Edward kicked it away and pointed the rifle at the Caucasian. The gunfire died down as suddenly as it erupted. The camp's survivors surrendered as the police took over.

Edward explored the area and found a bamboo enclosure at a corner of the compound. There, Edward found his wife with three other women. They were all stripped to their bras and panties. Edward consoled his wife; and took her to meet Jack.

As Edward walked with his wife, he noticed that the police had heaped the confiscated weapons near one of the huts. The prisoners were lined up according to race. There were a total of 53 prisoners. Three of the prisoners were US CIA paramilitary specialists. Twenty of the prisoners were local thugs; and the rest were Meo tribesmen from Laos. All the prisoners claimed that they were employees of Air America which operated out of Nakhon Phanom airport.

When Edward and Miriam found Jack, his left arm was in a makeshift sling. Jack told Edward and Miriam that he would be busy because the present situation involved national security. Jack then arranged for Edward and Miriam to be transported to the Phrae airport.

Operation Red Rock

On 22 November 1963, LBJ succeeded to the presidency and became the 36th US President, following the assassination of John F. Kennedy. LBJ was elected President in his own right, in the 1964 election. Johnson escalated US involvement in the Vietnam War, from 16,000 American advisors/soldiers in 1963, to 550,000 combat troops in early 1968. As a result, American casualties soared and the subsequent peace process bogged down. Later, Johnson did poorly in the 1968 New Hampshire primary; and he ended his bid for reelection. In 1968, Republican Richard Nixon ran for the presidency and was elected to succeed LBJ.

Nixon initially escalated America's involvement in the Vietnam War. He saw himself as a man wanting to end the war, but to end the war, Nixon carried it further and intensified it. Due to the general problem that the war was not definitely decided. North Vietnam as well as the US did not want to back down, they only got into talks on a peace plan because they wanted to win the war that way. Meanwhile, President Nixon sought to withdraw all US personnel from South-East Asia. However, Nixon anticipated that withdrawal would cause a military vacuum. This included US covert forces fighting secret wars in Laos and Cambodia. Hence, Nixon wanted the vacuum caused by the withdrawal of US covert forces to be filled by native Cambodian forces.

The Cambodian leader, Lon Nol, stubbornly resisted Nixon's diplomatic overtures to take up the slack. Lon Nol was anxious to retain US presence in the region; and was certain he had very little chance of survival, should Khmer Rouge and Vietnamese forces swarmed in, unhindered by US air power.

A plan was prepared at the highest levels of Nixon's administration, to create a covert team called "Team Red Rock." Team Red Rock was to secretly enter Cambodia's capital, Phnom Penh; and attack the airport, military and civil installations, wreaking as much havoc as possible. The plan called for the team to parachute into the outskirts of Phnom Penh, carrying captured North Vietnamese Army (NVA) "Sappers" with them. Taken in unarmed and alive, the Sappers would be "sacrificed" and their bodies left to be discovered by Cambodian forces. It was envisaged that a furious Lon Nol would assume North Vietnam was to blame. Thus, such an act would likely stiffen Lon Nol's backbone. With nowhere else to turn, the US puppet would urgently seek US hardware to strengthen his forces and continue the battle.

In December 1970, "Team Red Rock" was organized at Nakhon Phanom, Thailand. The Red Rock Team was composed of eight US Army Green Berets, three US Navy SEALs and two

CIA paramilitary specialists. Unknown to the team members, they would also be sacrificed by their President, to ensure that word of the operation never reached the light of day. A detachment of Montagnard tribesmen ("the Yards"), in the pay of the CIA, was assigned to liquidate every member of the Red Rock team.

The attack went successfully according to plan, but the team were suspicious of "the Yards." This foiled President Nixon's betrayal of the team. Using their knowledge of "escape and evasion" tactics, the team trekked towards the Vietnamese border, to be back in the safety of the US forces. Along the way, casualties thinned out their numbers until only eight of them remained. Soon, some were captured by NVA regulars and underwent hideous torture at the hands of Chinese and Russian interrogators. Ultimately, only two team members survived the ordeal.

The Pegasus File

Former CIA deep-cover agent, Gene "Chip" Tatum, was one of the survivors from Red Rock team. From 1986 to 1992, Tatum operated for a group which he called "Pegasus." The name "Pegasus" was a cover designation used by Tatum to protect himself against possible prosecution. Pegasus operated on behalf of the US and other governments, undertaking tasks that ranged from narcotics smuggling to assassinations.

There were several meetings that Tatum met with then Vice President Bush at the residence of his mother, Rose Bush, on Jupiter island. Jupiter island, measuring half a mile wide and nine miles long, was located at the Atlantic coast of Florida. The island's residents read like a "Who's Who" of the Anglo-American establishment. Many were closely connected to the intelligence apparatus; and some were also members of the secret Skull and Bones Society of the Masonic lodge, at Yale law school. Jupiter island boasts hyper-security. All vehicles were tracked by sensors placed in the roads. Every housekeeper, gardener and other non-residents were fingerprinted and registered.

The Pegasus group was an ultra-secret, international G7-run "hit team." The G7 began in 1975 as the Group of Six and included the countries of France, West Germany, Italy, Japan, United Kingdom, and United States. In the following year, the G7 was joined by Canada. Around 1983, the G7 took over 'Operation Gladio' which was the clandestine NATO operation in Europe. As such, Operation Gladio became international in nature. In the US, the Pegasus group's Gladio type operations in North and South America was directed by H. W. Bush who was assisted by a former Mossad agent, Amiram Nir. Hence, the Pegasus group activities became a joint CIA and Mossad operations. Of course, CIA and Mossad assets were utilized.

7

Birth Of The Promis Software

It was the year 1972, Edward was at the Medical City Dallas hospital with his newborn son. The first to congratulate Edward, was his colleague, Steve Dalton. Now that he became a father, Edward had the urge to take up a computer science course so that he could have a less risky job with a higher pay. Miriam was delighted and encouraged Edward to prepare for entry into a university.

Edward went to visit Clive Barker and Grant Thomson from the University of North Texas. Clive and Grant told Edward that he could take up an undergraduate course in Bachelor of Science (Computer Science) at the UNT Department of Computer Science and Engineering, 3940 North Elm Street, Denton, Texas. Through the patient guidance of Clive and Grant, Edward managed to meet all the requirements for entry into the undergraduate course in computer science, by 1974. At this time, Edward's son, Tom, was just two years old. Edward resigned from the Dallas Police Department to take up a full time course at the University of North Texas. Apart from his meager savings, Edward depended on Miriam's income for the next four years.

Upon Richard Nixon's resignation on 9 August 1974, Gerald Rudolph "Jerry" Ford became the 38th US President. One of his more controversial acts was to grant a presidential pardon to Richard Nixon for his role in the Watergate scandal. The Watergate affair began with the arrest of five men for breaking into the Democratic

National Committee (DNC) headquarters at the Watergate complex on 17 June 1972. These five burglars were Bernard L. Barker (former CIA operative), Virgilio R. Gonzales (former refugee from Cuba), James W. McCord (former FBI and CIA agent), Eugenio R. Martinez (CIA informer and former anti-Castro Cuban exile) and Frank A. Sturgis (CIA informer and anti-Castro radical). The objective of the burglary was to retrieve documents related to Daniel Ellsberg's Pentagon Papers which were mostly an indictment of the US Administration of Lyndon B. Johnson. This burglary was a CIA covert operation, to destroy any evidence that would link the Vietnam war to the golden triangle drug trade. However, Nixon's attempted cover-up of the Watergate scandal was also related to the involvement of the burglars in the JFK assassination. Thus, even Gerald Ford had a duty to the Illuminati, to 'pardon' Nixon and stop further leaks that might also implicate himself.

In the same year of Nixon's resignation, 1974, William Anthony Hamilton, former analyst with the National Security Agency and one time contract employee of the CIA, created a non-profit business called the Institute for Law and Social Research (Inslaw). Inslaw's original software product, Promis, was a database designed to handle papers and documents generated by law enforcement agencies and courts. Promis had the power to integrate innumerable databases regardless of their software languages, or regardless of their operating platforms. Promis was funded almost entirely by the Justice Department's Law Enforcement Assistance Administration (LEAA). On 1 January 1978, amendments to the Copyright Act of 1976 automatically conferred upon Inslaw as the author of Promis, five exclusive software copyrights. None of the copyright could be waived, except by explicit written waiver. The federal government negotiated licenses to use but not to modify or to distribute outside of the federal government, some but not all versions of Promis created after January 1978.

Edward persevered in his studies. The day of graduation came in 1978, Edward walked proudly up to the stage and collected his degree. Later, Edward went with Miriam and Tom to a restaurant, for a dinner celebration.

With his Bachelor of Science (Computer Science) degree, Edward applied for a job at the National Security Agency (NSA). His application and subsequent interview was successful; and he was employed by the NSA in the area of Information Systems Security.

In 1980, Ronald Wilson Reagan won both the Republican nomination and general election, defeating incumbent Jimmy Carter. In 1981, Edwin Meese, then an advisor to President Ronald Reagan, announced an $800 million budget in an effort to overhaul the computer systems of the Justice Department, the Federal Bureau of Investigation (FBI) and other law enforcement agencies. The following year, the Department of Justice (DoJ) awarded Inslaw a $9.6 million three year contract to implement a pilot Promis (Prosecutors Management Information Systems) program in 22 of the largest Offices of the US Attorneys using the older 16-bit architecture Prime version (IBM) which the government had a license to use. The contract between Inslaw and Justice quickly became embroiled for over two decades in bitter controversy. The conflict centered on whether the Justice Department owed Inslaw license fees for the newer 32-bit architecture VAX version, if the government substituted that version for the older 16-bit Prime version which was the subject in the original contract.

In February 1983, an Israeli government official, Dr. Ben Orr, made an appointment to visit Inslaw through the Justice Department's contract agent, Peter Videnieks. The visit was for a Promis presentation because the Israeli Ministry of Justice wanted to computerize its own prosecution offices. It was later discovered that the Israeli government official was not a prosecuting attorney, but was really Rafi Eitan, "Director of LAKAM, a super-secret agency in the Israeli Ministry of Defense responsible for collecting scientific and technical intelligence information from other countries through espionage."

After the Israeli meeting, the Justice Department obtained Inslaw's new 32-bit Enhanced Promis software from Inslaw. Consequently, the Implementation Contract was modified (1983 Modification 12 agreement); and there would be future negotiations on revised payment of license fees. A month later, the US government began finding fault with Inslaw's services. Each month, the government then withheld increasing amounts of payments due to Inslaw. The government not only failed to negotiate the payment of license fees as promised; but also claimed that Inslaw had developed the enhanced version with government funds and that it had provided the enhanced version voluntarily. By February 1985, the withheld payment was almost $1.8 million for Inslaw's implementation services, plus millions of dollars in the Old Promis license fees. Inslaw then filed for Chapter 11 bankruptcy protection.

Back Door To Fame And Fortune

The primary focus of some top-level individuals within the DoJ was to maintain international, covert intelligence operations, such as enabling Israeli signal intelligence to "surreptitiously access the computerized Jordanian dossiers on Palestinians." However, Inslaw contracts for the provision of Promis to Justice in 1982 and 1983, had nothing to do with tracking terrorist activities. Hamilton's suits charged that Reagan Administration officials, including Edwin Meese, pirated the software, modified it for intelligence and financial uses and made millions by selling it to the governments of Israel, Canada, Great Britain, Germany and other friendly nations. After the CIA created a "back door" into the program, Israel used its lifelong Mossad agent Robert Maxwell to sell the software to various "unfriendly" nations and then secretly retrieved priceless intelligence data. A 16 October 2001 FOX News report by correspondent Carl Cameron, reported that convicted spy, former FBI Agent Robert Hanssen, had provided a software program called Promis to Russian organized crime figures who in turn sold it to Osama bin Laden. This implied security breaches that might be helping the most wanted man in the world (namely Osama bin Laden). Osama's reported possession of Promis explained the alleged threatening messages that were received by President Bush while aboard Air Force One on 11th September 2001.

Michael Riconosciuto was an electronics and computer expert who alleged that he was directed by Earl Brian to adapt the PROMIS software for intelligence purposes. Riconosciuto confirmed that a copy of the PROMIS software was provided to him, by Earl Brian. Brian who owns United Press International (UPI) received pirated copies of PROMIS software, from Peter Videnieks, as a payoff for his part in the "October Surprise" that brought Reagan to power. A last minute deal with Iran to release the US hostages might earn incumbent Jimmy Carter enough votes, to win re-election in the 1980 presidential election. In "October Surprise," a secret deal was made by Reagan's close associates with Iran, to delay the release of US hostages. Videnieks was the Contract Officer who oversaw Inslaw Inc.'s Promis contract for the Management Division of the US Department of Justice. Previously, Videnieks was from the US Customs Service (Agency of the US federal government that collected import tariffs and performed other selected border security duties) where he oversaw contracts between that agency and Hadron, Inc., a company controlled by Edwin Meese and Earl Brian.

Israeli Mossad agent, Ari Ben Menashe, concurred with Riconosciuto's statements, saying Earl Brian had visited Israel in 1987, to demonstrate up-dated PROMIS software. During that meeting, Brian revealed that all US Intelligence agencies were using the software. The Israeli spy went on to explain that Riconosciuto's PROMIS modifications had a telecommunications "trapdoor." This trapdoor enabled US intelligence to eavesdrop on those organizations and nations that had purchased the illegal software. Altogether 88 nations had acquired the modified PROMIS, including Britain's intelligence and security services. In fact, the first intelligence use of PROMIS was in the British and US nuclear submarine fleet. Installed on Vax computers, the software was used to collect and disseminate vital intelligence between both allies. Former Deputy Director of the Mossad, Rafi Eitan, admitted the partnership between Israeli and US intelligence in selling to foreign intelligence agencies in excess of $500 million worth of licenses to a trojan horse version of Promis, in order to spy on these agencies.

According to Hamilton, with a staggering 570,000 lines of computer code, PROMIS could integrate innumerable databases without requiring any reprogramming. In essence, PROMIS could turn blind data into information. Converted to use by intelligence agencies, as had been alleged in interviews by ex-CIA and Israeli Mossad agents, PROMIS could be a powerful tracking device capable of monitoring intelligence operations, agents and targets, instead of just legal cases.

The House Committee reported investigative leads indicating that friends of the Reagan White House had been allowed to sell and to distribute Enhanced Promis both domestically and overseas for their personal financial gain and in support of the intelligence and foreign policy objectives of the United States.

Victims Of The Octopus

While seeking evidence for Riconosciuto relating to the Inslaw case, private investigator Larry Guerrin was killed in Mason County, Washington, in February 1987.

Lester Coleman, a former operative for the Defense Intelligence Agency, unveiled more aspects of the shadowy Octopus, in his book "Trail of the Octopus." Following his public revelations, Coleman and his family fled to Sweden after death threats from US intelligence community. His story focuses on covert activities that resulted in the Lockerbie plane disaster. Aboard Pan Am Flight 103, were a team of US intelligence agents—known as the McKee team—returning home to reveal illegal CIA narcotics smuggling run by George W. Bush, from Lebanon to the US. As a result, Pan Am Flight 103 was destroyed by an explosive device, killing all 243 passengers and 16 crew members, on Wednesday, 21 December 1988; and blamed on Libya. Coleman revealed that the Lockerbie flight was used as a conduit for narcotics smuggling.

A freelance journalist, Danny Casolaro, had been investigating a shadowy group he called "The Octopus." The Octopus consisted of factions within the intelligence community (such as the CIA and Mossad), the Mafia and high level government figures which had teamed up to engage in illegal, but highly profitable activities. Behind the veil of national secrecy, these activities included widespread narcotic smuggling, gun running, money laundering and manipulations of stock and financial markets. All these activities were now facilitated by enhanced versions of Inslaw's PROMIS software.

On 31 January 1991, the body of Alan D. Standorf was found in the back seat of a car parked at the Washington National Airport. Standorf was a source of information to Casolaro; and had been introduced to him by Riconosciuto. Standorf who was an electronic intelligence employee for the National Security Agency, was a key source for some of the information linking the Justice Department to the various scandals (including theft of Inslaw's Promis).

On 19 June 1991, Alan Michael May was found dead in his San Francisco home. May had reportedly been involved with Michael Riconosciuto and the movement of $40 million in bribe money to the Iranians, in the operation known as the "October Surprise."

Danny Casolaro was probably aware that the Octopus being a deadly creature which had publicly killed JFK, would terminate the live of anyone who stood in its way. Furthermore, this creature had evolved into a cyborg (due to enhanced version of Promis), with the ability to operate in a virtual world of its own.

Members of the "Octopus," included highly placed figures in both the Reagan and Bush administrations and powerful individuals within the US and Israel intelligence community. Casolaro also had evidence that linked these people to senior figures in organised crime. All three parties operated together, in perpetrating massive swindles and engaging in widespread political fix-it. Central to the many activities of the "Octopus" that Casolaro unearthed, was the theft of a software package known as PROMIS. A final meeting with a new "source" would wrap the explosive story up. Despite recent death threats, he journeyed to a motel in Martinsburg, West Virginia, to meet his informant. The next day, Saturday, 10 August 1991, Casolaro was found dead in the bathtub of his motel room. His wrists were slashed open a dozen times. Local police officers were quick to conclude suicide. His briefcase containing sheaf's of documents relating to his story were missing. Without notifying his family, Casolaro's body was illegally embalmed, impeding subsequent autopsy.

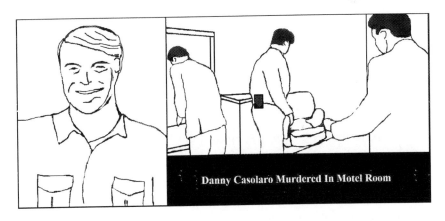

Danny Casolaro Murdered In Motel Room

Danny Casolaro Murdered In Motel Room

The London headquarters of the collapsed bank, BCCI, used a modified version of PROMIS to track money and letters of credit on behalf of intelligence agencies. Evidence provided by Ari Ben Menashe and others claim that British publisher, Robert Maxwell, distributed PROMIS on behalf of Mossad. Maxwell's suspicious death was related to the shadowy activities of Casolaro's "Octopus." BCCI was widely implicated in narcotics smuggling and money laundering.

Mossad had stolen the most important piece of software in the US arsenal. Mossad's spy, Maxwell, was given the job of marketing the stolen Promis software. The Mossad had inserted into the software, a device which enabled them to track the use any purchaser made of it. Sitting in Israel, Mossad would know exactly what was going on inside all the intelligence services that bought it. In all, Maxwell sold it to 42 countries, including China and Soviet Bloc nations. But his greatest triumph was selling it to Los Alamos, the very heart of the US nuclear defense system. With the money, Maxwell spent lavishly and lost money on deals. The more he lost, the more he tried to claw money from the banks. Then he demanded money from Mossad for past services, he wanted a quick fix of £400 million to bale him out of his financial difficulties. Maxwell was contacted. He was told to fly to Gibraltar, go aboard the Lady Ghislaine and sail to the Canary Islands. There at sea, he would receive his £400million quick fix in the form of a banker's draft. Maxwell did as he was told. On the night of 4 November 1991, the Lady Ghislaine, one of the world's biggest yachts, was at sea. The Mossad death squad had cast an electronic net over the yacht to block all radio transmissions. The security cameras on board were switched off. A small boat came alongside. On board were four dark suited men. Three men scrambled onto the yacht. They found Maxwell; and two men held Maxwell. The third man plunged a syringe into his neck behind his ear. A measured dose of nerve agent was injected. Robert Maxwell was immobilized. Then, he was lowered off the deck into the water.

The FBI went to Ruby Ridge looking for a neighbor of Randy Weaver, Barry Kumnick's father. Weaver refused to spy on Kumnick for the FBI; and was getting in the way of their search. Actually, the feds were on the trail of Barry, a computer programmer who had gone missing with a pirated copy of a twice-modified, highly sensitive software package originally called "Promis," which the DoJ had virtually stolen from a company called "Inslaw." The subsequent 1992 siege of Ruby Ridge, resulted in the death of Weaver's son Sammy, his wife Vicki, and Deputy US Marshal William Francis

Degan. Many people had died (been murdered or were 'suicided') or were imprisoned in the fallout from this case.

Suspicion grew around the speculation that the feds thought that the missing Promis software (which Kumnick had modified for the DoJ, with artificial intelligence for profiling) was in the Davidians' computer system, at their Mt Carmel community in Waco. On 28 February 1993, BATF agents in National Guard helicopters zoomed in on the Branch Davidians' church and home, at Mount Carmel Center, with guns blazing, like a US raid of a Vietnamese village in that far off war. The raid went badly. Consequently, six Branch Davidians and four agents were killed. After fifty one days standoff, the US Justice Department approved a plan to use CS gas against those barricaded inside. Tanks carrying the CS gas entered the compound. Later that day, fire broke out; and all seventy-four men, women and children inside perished. A computer programmer, Jeff Little, was one of the Waco victims. Jeff was handling the Davidians' computer which was thought to contain a modified Promis software in its electronic memory. On Feb 1993, Eric Arron Lighter (Federal Witness) revealed the connection between the events of Inslaw (PROMIS SOFTWARE), Ruby Ridge and the events that occurred at Waco.

Barry R. Kumnick, a brilliant computer engineer with high security clearance, developed an artificial intelligence software suite that would dramatically enhance PROMIS. Missing since 1991, Kumnick's enhancement software, known as "Brainstorm" was discovered, along with his personal possessions and working papers, in five storage crates during an auction. Allegedly, Brainstorm had a powerful element of personality profiling added to PROMIS, enabling it to track individuals by predicting their thoughts and future actions. In a letter to his sister, Kumnick said the software would be extremely dangerous in the wrong hands. The US government offered him $25million for the package and then, like Inslaw, reneged on the deal.

Journalist, Paul Wilcher, was investigating possible government involvement in October Surprise and the Inslaw PROMIS story. By May 1993, he told friends that his information had gone "beyond" Casolaro's. On 23 June 1993, he was found dead in the bathroom of his apartment. Wilcher's investigation records were missing. FBI and CIA personnel were quickly on the scene. As with Casolaro, Wilcher's bathroom was thoroughly cleaned the next day. His body was cremated before identification was independently confirmed; and without complete forensic examination, cause of death could not be established.

Vincent Foster, a White House deputy counsel and long-time personal friend of Bill and Hillary Clinton, was found on 20 July 1993, dead of a gunshot wound to the mouth—a death ruled suicide. Despite Dr. Haut's signed report confirming the existence of a second wound to Vincent Foster's neck, radio host Rush Limbaugh to this very day refers to Vincent Foster's death as a suicide. Foster was working on a NSA project about the PROMIS software used to track international money flows. During the 1995 US House hearings on Waco, someone in the Texas Governor's office gave Vince Foster's phone number to contact. The hearings revealed that the only document found in Foster's Waco file was a memorandum that Foster was forwarding "Waco, the Big Lie" (a videotape charging government conspiracy) to the Treasury Department.

8
The Beginning Of ZAT

By end January 1991, Edward Field had worked in the NSA for almost thirteen years. When the body of Alan D. Standorf was found in a car parked at the Washington National Airport, Edward was shocked that an employee of NSA was murdered. Edward knew that Alan was involved in a special software engineering and application project. Edward had met Alan a few times at in-house seminars conducted by NSA. To Edward, Alan was just a normal person doing a professional job for NSA. However, Edward was aware that Alan had been talking to a freelance investigative reporter by the name of Joseph Daniel Casolaro.

Although Edward had left the police force for more than a decade, he was curious about Joseph D. Casolaro. Hence, Edward asked Miriam who was now working for the Baltimore Sun whether she had heard about Casolaro. Miriam told Edward that she heard about Casolaro doing an investigation on a scandal involving a software developed by a previous intelligence analyst from the NSA. Edward was extremely interested and thought that he would ask other NSA colleagues about the software. After a week, Edward pieced together some information about a previous NSA employee by the name of Bill Hamilton. Bill Hamilton was previously working in NSA as an intelligence analyst assigned to the research and development unit, in developing a computer database program which would interface with other computers. Edward was excited by his finding and tried to find out more about Bill Hamilton. According to some colleagues, Bill Hamilton was supported by the US government to start a company called Inslaw Incorporated. The database software that Bill Hamilton developed was copyrighted as PROMIS (which stands for Prosecutors Management Information Systems) and leased the rights for its use to the Justice Department. Immediately, Edward smelt a rat because any system developed within the NSA should belong to it.

Edward concluded that there were persons within the US government, NSA and the Justice Department who were involved from the beginning, in the formation of Inslaw Incorporated.

Edward guessed from experience gained in his previous investigation of his sister's murder that there was a formidable group of people behind Inslaw Incorporated, just as there was a formidable group of people behind the big event.

Edward's curiosity got the better of him. Edward found out that since February 1985, the US government had withheld payments of $1.77 million in costs and fees; and Inslaw was forced into bankruptcy. This meant there was another formidable group that was in direct conflict with the group behind Inslaw.

Edward found out that in 1981, Edwin Meese, then an advisor to President Ronald Reagan, announced an $800 million budget in an effort to overhaul the computer systems of the Justice Department, the FBI and other law enforcement agencies. It was in 1982, that the Justice Department signed a $10 million contract with Inslaw, to install PROMIS into the offices of 42 US attorneys. Also in 1982, Earl Brian was appointed to a White House post to advise on health-care issues. In the White House, Brian reported directly to Ed Meese. During this time, Brian arranged White House tours to woo investors in his government contracting company, Hadron Inc. which was a competitor to Inslaw Inc. Hadron Inc. sought to obtain the rights to Inslaw's PROMIS software and the government contract. In fact, Hadron Chairman Dominic Laiti had previously attempted to purchase the software from Inslaw, but Hamilton refused the offer.

Through Edward's persistent investigations, he found that Brian had suspected connections with Director of Central Intelligence, William J. Casey, and Israeli intelligence community covert operations. As Inslaw sought refuge in Chapter 11 in 1985, Justice Department officials pressured the IRS to force Inslaw into Chapter 7 liquidation. Hence, it was clear to Edward that the formidable force opposing Inslaw's group consisted of Edwin Meese, people in NSA, Earl Brian, Hadron Inc., William Casey, agents in CIA, Justice Department officials and agents in Mossad.

In mid February 1991, Edward called Danny Casolaro on the phone, to talk about Alan Standorf. As Edward had introduced himself as an employee of NSA, Danny agreed to a short telephone discussion. Danny told Edward that Alan was previously introduced to him by Michael J. Riconosciuto. Edward asked Danny about Michael Riconosuito. Danny informed that Michael was a very talented scientist who worked as a project manager for the Wackenhut Company, a security company that was a known CIA front. According to Danny, regarding Michael's work for Wackenhut, Michael had engaged in modification of the proprietary PROMIS computer software product, between 1983 and 1984. The copy of PROMIS on which Michael worked, came from the Department of Justice. Earl Brian made it available to Michael through Wackenhut after acquiring it from Peter Videnieks. Peter was then a Department of Justice contracting official, with responsibility for the PROMIS software. Michael created a "back door" into the Promis software. This would enable the trackers of other intel agencies using PROMIS to be tracked by the CIA.

Being a senior computer executive of NSA's Information System Security, Edward decided to check on the digital files stored by Alan Standorf. It was easy for Edward to access Alan's files because of the nature of Edward's work at NSA. Within two hours, Edward was able to view all of Alan's files. Edward even came across a version of the Promis software among Alan's files. Edward guessed that Alan had obtained a copy of Promis from Michael. Edward was engrossed with the copy of Promis. Later, a database file called 'Lonol Red

Rock' was located in computer memory. In this file, Edward found sixteen names. The first name on the list was General Alexander Haig followed by CIA Saigon Chief William Colby. The third listed was radio operator Gene Tatum. The remaining fourteen personals were listed as US Army Green Berets, Navy SEALs and CIA paramilitary specialists. The 'Lonol Red Rock' database also described the location of operation 'Red Rock,' to be in Phnom Penh. Edward then remembered his honeymoon trip in Thailand. At that time, Edward met Jack Bhumipol who told him that the US conducted secret wars in Laos and Cambodia, from a base at Nakhon Phanom, Thailand. Here at last, Edward had access to a database with such information related to US secret operations in other countries.

Edward realized that with the copy of Promis in Alan's files, he could crack the code for backdoor access to similar Promis databases worldwide. However, his knowledge was limited; and he needed someone with superior knowledge of computer software programming. To Edward, a suitable person for such a task would be his long time colleague, Steven Green. Steven was a computer whiz who was a successful hacker. Steven considered obtaining unauthorized access into databases of other organizations a challenge akin to mountain climbing. Nevertheless, NSA was not aware of Steven's prowess because after Steven gained access into the servers of other institutions, he was always careful not to leave any traces.

Edward confided with Steven during lunch, about Alan's files. As soon as he heard about the Promis software, Steven's face lit up. Still, Steven cautioned Edward that CIA agents could use the backdoor access of Alan's Promis software, to monitor activities within NSA. Edward realized the potential two-way flow of data between NSA and CIA. Both Steven and Edward were very excited.

The Brotherhood Of Blood

The creation of Promis provided a tool for three families to form a coalition in Cyber space that would unleash world chaos, transfer billions of petrodollar wealth into their pockets and usher in the New World Order.

After 1985, the families of Vlad Dracula Ashkenazi Jews, al-Saud Crypto Jews and bin Laden Crypto Jews formed a virtual enterprise of mercenaries that would mount Gladio type false flag operations.

The head of the Vlad Dracula family was H. W. Bush who was able to control the CIA. Thus, the virtual enterprise of mercenaries were stored as a database in the CIA's computer server system. The human assets of the CIA would be listed in this database. Transfers of money to fund the false flag operations would be digital and based on information transfers between various banks. As far as possible, espionage to obtain useful information for mounting the false flag operations would involve the hacking of computer systems from governments and organizations. As such, the virtual world and the real world would be merged into one.

Steven experimented with cracking the backdoor access of Alan's Promis software. It was a difficult but challenging task. After two days Steven scored a success; and Edward was elated. Both Edward and Steven could hardly wait to try a backdoor access into the CIA's Promis software.

It was early March 1991 that Steven gained backdoor access into the CIA's Promis software. A database file labeled ZAT-911 was discovered. In the file was a list of mainly Middle Eastern names. First on the list was the name Tim Ossman. Next on the list was Mohammed Atta. There were about ten men on the list. The last man on the list was Adam Gadahn. Edward scribbled the first two names and the last name onto a slip of paper, to do further research on their backgrounds. Suddenly, a message from the CIA appeared in the NSA computer. Steven opened the message file; and Edward looked at the message which read: "This is Jim Davis. You guys are taking a big risk. Let us discuss."

Edward and Steven did not answer the message, but discussed among themselves. Steven thought that it was not a risk to meet up with Jim Davis because they were suppose to monitor NSA security issues. Furthermore, they know that Jim Davis was a CIA employee and probably working in the information processing department. Edward concurred and they left a message for Jim Davis to call them at NSA.

Jim did call; and Edward made an appointment for Jim to meet at the restaurant of Northeast Garden Inn in Laurel, Maryland. It was a convenient spot between CIA headquarters at Langley in McLean, Virginia and NSA headquarters at Fort George G. Meade, Maryland. On 6th March 1991, Steven and Edward met Jim at the appointed place and time. Edward immediately recognized Jim Davis as Jack Smith. Jack Smith also recognized Edward Field. Jim told Edward that he assumed one of his other identities in Panama, after the episode in Texas. Jim only returned to the US two years ago.

Edward told Jim that due to the murder of Alan Standorf, they stumbled onto Alan's copy of the Promis software. In his capacity as senior computer executive of NSA's Information System Security, Edward maintained that it was his duty to check if NSA's Information System had been compromised. Jim replied that to his knowledge, the CIA had never given a copy of Promis to Alan. Edward stated that the Promis software belonged to Inslaw; and both the CIA and NSA had unauthorized copies of Promis.

Jim's face was red with embarrassment, but he quickly explained his real intent of meeting up with Edward and Steven. Jim informed that he discovered that the CIA was really working for a secret organization known as the Illuminati. The Illuminati was a group of international Satanists who controlled the Secret or Inner government of the US, as well as every other major governments in the world. In the 1960's, the CIA set up a covert operation called 'The Finders.' This operation involved the kidnapping of children, for purposes of prostitution, pornography, high tech weaponry experimental abuse, mind control abuse, child slave labor for secret underground facilities, white sex slavery and the satanic ritual murder of thousands of American children snatched from the streets and playgrounds of America by CIA agents. According to Jim, the kidnapping of children was still being carried out.

Edward was not surprised that children were kidnapped for satanic ritual murders because that was what happened to his sister. Based on his own experience, Edward opined that the members of the Illuminati were Jews.

Steven suggested that they should expose CIA schemes that were against US interests. Jim and Edward concurred. Edward then showed Jim the three names which were included in a CIA database file labeled ZAT-911. Jim replied that Tim Ossman, Mohammed Atta and Adam Gadahn were all CIA assets. Jim informed that all three men were Crypto Jews which meant that they were secretly Jews, but appeared to be Muslims. Jim also divulged that CIA agent, Michael Riconosciuto and former FBI head of the Los Angeles field office, Ted Gunderson, had met with Tim Ossman, at the Hilton Hotel in Sherman Oaks, California, in late Spring of 1986. This meeting was also attended by Ralph Olberg who procured American weapons and technology for the Afghan rebels, through a front called Management Sciences for Health. According to Jim, Michael proposed assisting the mujahedeen with MANPADs (Man Portable Air Defense Systems) by obtaining the basic components for the unassembled Chinese 107 MM rocket system. These could be reconfigured into a man-portable, shoulder fired, anti-aircraft guided missile system; and produced in Pakistan at the Pakistan Ordinance Works.

After the meeting, Edward made a mental note to call on both Michael Riconosciuto and Ted Gunderson.

It was the first time that Edward heard about Ted Gunderson. At home, Edward asked Miriam about Ted Gunderson. Miriam told Edward that Ted was FBI Special Agent In Charge and Head of the

Los Angeles FBI Field Office. After Ted retired from the FBI in 1979, he set up his private investigation firm, Ted L. Gunderson and Associates, in Santa Monica, California. Ted began to investigate cases of satanic murder activity, after becoming convinced of the innocence of a young Army medical doctor, Dr. Jeffrey R. MacDonald, who was falsely convicted in August 1979, for the satanic murder of his wife and two young daughters. Gunderson eventually found a woman who corroborated McDonald's story and admitted she was among the group who entered McDonald's home and committed the murders. The court discounted her confession and the woman was later killed. There were obvious irregularities committed by the government in the McDonald case; and Ted knew that these were meant to obstruct the capture of the satanic ritual participants. Otherwise, there would be exposure of highly placed government and civilian individuals who were involved. In November 1988, investigation by the FBI and IRS of a black man named Larry King who as president of the Franklin Credit Union in Omaha, Nebraska, was involved in millions of missing funds, led to the discovery of a satanic child abuse/sex slave ring. Ted made public the details of this case. About 80 youngsters made allegations concerning sexual abuse, forced prostitution, and cult activities, including the human sacrifice of small children and babies at satanic rituals.

Two weeks went by, after the meeting between Jim, Edward and Steven. On 21 March 1991, Michael Riconosciuto filed an affidavit before a House judiciary committee investigating the bankruptcy case of Inslaw Inc. versus the US Government. Michael filed the affidavit because he was under suspicion for illegally modifying the Promis software developed by Inslaw Inc. In the affidavit, Michael declared that he had been under the direction of Earl Brian who was the Director of Hadron Inc. which was a competitor of Inslaw Inc. Michael disclosed that the copy of Promis in Earl's possession came from Peter Videnieks who was the Department of Justice contract manager. Eight days later, Michael was jailed on a fabricated charge of drug manufacturing and distribution of methamphetamine between 1987 and 1989.

Michael's affidavit was related to an affidavit of 17 February 1991 by Ari Ben Menashe who described his 12 years service for the Government of Israel in foreign Intelligence. Ari provided an eyewitness account of a presentation to an Israeli intelligence agency in 1987 at Tel Aviv, by Earl Brian of the United States. According to Ari's affidavit, Brian stated in his presence that he had acquired the property rights to the PROMIS computer software; and that as of 1987, all US intelligence agencies, including the Defense Intelligence Agency, the Central Intelligence Agency and the National Security Agency, were using the PROMIS computer software. In his affidavit, Ben Menashe further stated that Brian had completed a sale of the PROMIS computer software to Israel in 1987.

On 3 April 1991, Jim, Steven and Edward met again. Jim informed that George H. W. Bush and son George W. Bush had financial and satanic cult links with drug trafficking through the Brownsville/ Matamoros area. Brownsville in the US near the Mexican border, was just above Matamoros, Mexico. Edward was amazed at how Zionist elements had made the US into a cesspool of satanic evil and death. The three of them concluded that the database labeled ZAT-911 immediately linked Tim Ossman with Michael Riconosciuto and Ted Gunderson which then was connected to the Promis software. The Promis episode exposed the people within the US government and then finally to Israel. Edward, Steven and Jim pondered how the persons listed in the ZAT-911 database would be related to one another.

All three decided to meet Ted Gunderson for more information on the Promis episode. Jim was tasked with contacting Ted Gunderson; and making arrangements for their meeting.

9

The World Of Tim Ossman

I t was 30 April 1991 when Jim, Steven and Edward met with Ted Gunderson at the café of Fairmont Miramar Hotel Santa Monica near Ocean road California. After the normal introductions, Jim told Ted that they were investigating the events that were related to the PROMIS software, when they came across the information of the PROMIS software modifications by Michael Riconosciuto. Jim explained to Ted that they were aware that he and Riconosciuto had met Tim Ossman.

Ted stated that he and Riconosciuto were both engaged in a classified CIA operation with the mujahedeens, to test new biological weapons in the Afghan war against the Soviet Union. Tim Ossman was to produce a research report on the effectiveness of the new weapons, complete with photos.

Edward was surprised and asked Ted what his previous status as FBI agent got anything to do with the CIA. Ted was hesitant to reply. Jim answered Edward, "The CIA, the FBI, the Mafia, the Dallas Police Department and every major US Police Department were all under the control of Francis Cardinal Spellman until 1967. Francis Cardinal Spellman was Jesuit trained and was a personal friend of the secret cold-warrior, Montini, Pius VI. In fact, former FBI Deputy Director was Knight of Malta, Cartha Deke DeLoach." Ted nodded and said, "The CIA and the FBI sometimes operate joint projects."

Suddenly, Edward realized the identity of the ultimate organization behind JFK's assassination. The thought of JFK's assassination, reminded Edward of his previous investigations on Lee Harvey Oswald, during his previous job in the Dallas Police Department. Several years after Oswald's murder, Edward learnt that Lee Harvey Oswald was the bodyguard of Judyth Vary Baker who was involved in developing cancer-causing monkey viruses for the CIA. This secret research was done in an underground medical laboratory located in David Ferrie's apartment at Louisiana Avenue Parkway in New Orleans. Of course, this information was not of any use to Edward by then.

Edward asked Ted, "Are the biological weapons being tested by the mujahedeens, anything to do with cancer-causing monkey viruses?" This time Ted was surprised. Ted cautiously answered Edward, "That was only a part of the biological weapons program, but other types of biological weapons were also tested. Returning to the purpose of our meeting, I wish to tell you that the Promis software modifications by Michael Riconosciuto was given to Tim Ossman for field testing."

Steven was interested and asked Ted, "What do you mean by field testing." Ted answered, "Well! You must understand that I am not a professional in information technology. I'll try to answer you in layman's terms. The modified version of the Promis software with its backdoor access is very useful for tracking individuals and organizations. It can even monitor electronic banking transactions, easing covert money transfer operations. The sky's the limit with what one can do with this kind of software." Ted paused and continued, "Tim Ossman is a CIA asset who is out in the Afghan battlefield fighting a guerilla war with the Soviets. This kind of software will be useful for him, to gain intelligence information from Soviet databases; and engage in cyber warfare as well. The CIA have also provided him with IT professionals."

Steven whistled and said, "I can see how testing its capabilities in a covert operation will be extremely useful. Still, our colleague, Alan Standorf, was murdered over the Promis software."

Ted said, "Sadly, we are dealing with a formidable and dangerous group of people who are engaging in various criminal activities. Having a copy of the Promis software will enable one to gain access into the databases of this group. Who knows what will be exposed!"

Edward asked Ted, "Do you know if they have infiltrated their people into the CIA and the FBI?" Ted answered, "Knight of Malta and a top FBI executive, Cartha Deke DeLoach, is an example. The "father of the CIA" was William Donovan, WWII OSS chief who was a Knight of Malta and the recipient of the Grand Cross of the Order of St. Sylvester. Other top CIA operatives, such as James J. Angleton, the Buckley brothers, Nelson Rockefeller, Reinhard Gehlen and George H. W. Bush, were also Knights of Malta. In fact, the CIA might as well be called the Catholic Intelligence Agency."

Edward said, "We know that these people are also members of satanic cults." Ted replied, "That is why I am investigating cases involving satanic ritual murders!"

Jim asked Ted, "Is the CIA involved?" Ted stated, "The CIA had a Washington D.C. group called the Finders that abduct children for mind control experiments, sexual abuse and satanic ritual sacrifices." Jim answered, "We are aware of the Finders group."

Edward said, "I suppose that white sex slavery would be part of the mind control experiments, sexual abuse and satanic ritual sacrifices." Ted answered, "Some of these victims come from broken families or foster homes; and have undergone further sexual abuse to create trauma, under the CIA's MK Ultra program which is now replaced by the Monarch program. Norma Jeane Mortenson (alias Marilyn Monroe) is rumored to be an example." Edward reflected upon Ted's information and exclaimed, "In that case, Marilyn Monroe might be murdered before JFK's assassination, to prevent any accidental information leak."

Ted revealed that he had been investigating the Masonic Muslim group also referred to as the Muslim brotherhood. According to Ted, many Masonic Muslims were Crypto Jews. Hence, they secretly worshipped Satan, just as what the Freemasons did because both groups were cults originating from the Kabbalah which was part of Judaism. Ted explained that the Muslim Brotherhood investigation was related to his monitoring of the activities by the CIA's Finders team.

Edward said, "In connection with our investigation of the PROMIS software, we found a CIA database file labeled ZAT-911. Tim Ossman is listed in ZAT-911." Ted replied, "I know what you are getting at. I do suspect that Tim is a member of the Muslim Brotherhood. The Muslim Brotherhood is based on mystical Sufism. Like western Freemasonry, there is a large overlap between Kabalistic and Sufic magical practice."

Ted paused to sip some coffee and continued, "Currently, the Muslim Brotherhood is funded by the al-Saud Crypto Jews and bin Laden Crypto Jews. A branch of the Muslim Brotherhood is based at the Mosque of Islamic Brotherhood Inc. in Harlem, at 55 Saint Nicholas Avenue, New York. My contact is making arrangements for me and others, to observe a Muslim Brotherhood secret ceremony in New York."

Jim took up the offer, "Can we join you?" Ted nodded and said, "I'll let you know about the arrangements."

In mid-May 1991, Edward, Jim and Steven met Ted and his contact near the intersection of St. Nicholas Avenue and W 113th St Neighborhoods at uptown, Manhattan. Ted's contact led them to a manhole cover. Upon opening the manhole cover, they climbed down a steel ladder which led them to a sewerage tunnel, 15 meters underground.

Ted's contact took out a flashlight and led them through a maze of tunnels. After sometime, all of them were lost with the exception of Ted's contact. Suddenly, Ted's contact stopped and told them that they were below the vicinity of the Mosque of Islamic Brotherhood Inc. Ted's contact opened a steel door at the tunnel wall; and all of them entered a hall. At one end of the hall, they could hear the muffled sounds of chanting. As Ted's contact led them to the source of the chantings, they saw a dark corridor. They then followed Ted's contact down the corridor. As they walked down the corridor, the chants became louder. Finally, they reached a heavy oak door. Ted's contact motioned them to arm themselves and they brought out their handguns. Ted's contact switched off his flashlight and darkness surrounded them.

Ted's contact opened the oak door slowly, to reveal a dimly lit room. They stealthily followed Ted's contact behind some pillars. As their eyes became accustomed to the dimly lit room, they saw a huge idol with the head of a goat. There were at least twenty hooded figures and they were all chanting.

Suddenly the chanting stopped. A bearded man with a black turban and a dark cloak entered the room and stood in front of the idol. Two muscular men dragged a young boy to the bearded man. The young boy was crying uncontrollably and let out a yell, "Mummy!"

In a flash, the bearded man whisked out a crescent shaped knife and slit the boy's throat. The boy's body went limp; and the muscular men quickly placed him faced down onto an altar. A hooded figure placed a flask below the throat of the boy, as blood flowed out from the wound.

Edward was angry as he remembered his sister's fate. Edward sprang out from behind a pillar and shouted, "Enough!" The worshippers turned and looked in Edward's direction. Two of the worshippers dashed towards Edward who fired his pistol into their heads; and they crumpled to the floor.

The room was in mayhem and most of the worshippers ran towards the exits. Ted, Jim, Steven and Ted's contact showed themselves from behind the pillars. Three worshippers and the two muscular men reached for their firearms and a gun battle erupted. It lasted less than two minutes; and all three worshippers and the two muscular men were shot. Edward and Jim managed to arrest the bearded man. Jim called out to the bearded man, "Who are you?" The bearded man replied, "I am Imam Ibrahim Hakki." Ted's contact quickly handcuffed the Imam. Steven demanded from the Imam, "Show us the exit!"

Imam Ibrahim Hakki walked towards the exit door with Edward and Steven following closely behind. Jim said, "Ted and I will contact the police. The rest of you can leave." Edward and Steven immediately dashed up a spiral staircase. It was a big effort to climb to the top of the staircase. When they reached the top, Edward and Steven were exhausted.

Edward and Steven found themselves in a secluded part of a mosque. They ran towards the sounds of footsteps and shouting. Edward caught a glimpse of two hooded figures making their way to a huge door. Edward motioned Steven; and both of them dashed through the door. They found themselves stepping into a narrow dark alley. Towards the left, they saw two men in the distance discarding some dark robes with hoods.

Edward and Steven waited until the two men had discarded their dark robes and continued walking. Then, Edward and Steven followed close behind, through a labyrinth of dark alleys. Eventually, they emerged in a street of Harlem. They saw the two men boarding a cab; and quickly hailed another cab. They instructed the cab driver to follow the front cab.

Finally, the front cab stopped at Freeport, New York. Edward saw the two men boarding a cruise ship called 'The Golden Horseshoe.' Edward and Steven decided not to board the vessel; but to check details of the cruise ship in their office.

The Masonic Web

Edward and Steven investigated the cruise ship called 'The Golden Horseshoe.' It was a casino cruise ship belonging to Adam Ruben who was suspected of being funded by Jack Abramoff. There were reports that Jack Abramoff had ties with the Buffalo, New York Cosa Nostra mob, operating in Canada under the reign of Montreal-based Joseph Bonanno.

It was a shock to Edward that Masonic Muslims had ties with the Mafia. In fact, the bagman for all false flag operations in the US, was Mossad agent Jack Abramoff; and evidence led even to the involvement of the American Turkish Council. Historically, Turkey was invaded by Crypto Jews such as Judeo-Bolsheviks working with Freemason Jew Mustafa Kemal (Ataturk).

Edward called Jim on the telephone and informed about the two Masonic Muslims boarding a casino cruise ship owned by Adam Ruben. Jim told Edward that Imam Ibrahim Hakki was arrested by the police, for the ritualistic killing of a boy. However, for some unknown reason, Imam Ibrahim Hakki was quietly released. Edward immediately concluded that there was a secret powerful group that supported the activities of the Masonic Muslims. Edward then realized that the Middle Eastern name list labeled ZAT-911, were those of Masonic Muslims who were supported by powerful Jewish and US organizations, such as Mossad and CIA.

Edward suddenly had the bigger picture of what was happening to his country. Beginning with the savage murder of his sister, there was a web of formidable organizations that was gaining ground in the US by covert operations, both within the country and in other nations. The common characteristic of all these organizations was their worship of Satan.

Edward knew that more events would be unleashed upon the US, in time to come. The database file labeled ZAT-911 was for a future event. Edward was sure that many US citizens would be killed by the evil web of secret organizations. In his vague memory, Edward recalled that JFK had ever spoken about secret organizations, just a few months before his assassination. JFK did his best as President of USA, to claim back control of US destiny by its own people. Now, it is up to Edward and a few others to be on the alert; and defend his own country from being taken over by covert operations.

10

Epilogue

On the morning of Tuesday 2 July 1991, Edward received an urgent phone call from Jim. Jim made an appointment to meet with Edward and Steven, around 3.00 pm the same day at the restaurant of Northeast Garden Inn in Laurel, Maryland. Both Edward and Steven met Jim at the agreed rendezvous. Jim quickly told Edward and Steven that he heard some CIA agents had made arrangements with Mossad and the Masonic Muslims, to bomb a landmark in New York with a special device.

Edward asked Jim whether he knew the names of members in these groups. Jim did not know because it was not an official CIA operation. However, Jim did hear that Tim Ossman was involved.

It was decided that Edward would contact freelance journalist, Danny Casolaro, while Jim would contact Ted Gunderson, to find out the latest information on Tim Ossman. Meanwhile, Steven would search the CIA database with NSA's copy of the Promis software.

Edward called up Casolaro on 3 July 1991. Edward told Casolaro about an impending terrorist bomb attack on a US landmark. Edward also informed that Tim Ossman would be involved. Casolaro opined that based on his investigation of the shadowy group which he called "The Octopus," there would be a series of false flag operations in the US. Casolaro pointed out that the London connection would be the ultimate power behind these attacks. As such, there were dots linking the Jesuits to the London connection. It was Knight of Malta,

Henry R. Luce who bought the Zapruder Film for US$150,000 and then altered the record of President Kennedy's CIA/FBI/Secret Service/Mafia assassination. Henry Luce's CIA technicians cut out two seconds of the film when the presidential limousine came to a complete stop on Elm Street, at which time the driver then shot JFK in the head simultaneously with others. At the same time, the storm drain shooter shot at Kennedy but wounded John B. Connally instead.

Edward asked Casolaro whether he heard anything about a special bomb device. Casolaro reported that Michael Riconosciuto talked about his development of an Electro-Hydrodynamic Gaseous Fuel Device which could achieved near-atomic explosive yields. Casolaro informed that Michael Riconoscuito claimed that this bomb device could be miniaturized.

Edward was excited about Casolaro's disclosures and could hardly wait to find out what Jim and Steven had discovered.

Edward went to check with Steven, on any new information posted in the CIA database. Steven told Edward that the ZAT-911 database file was listed with an assignment called project New Gladio Phase 2.

Edward called Jim about the meeting with Ted Gunderson. Over the phone, Jim briefed Edward that according to Ted, Tim Ossman is residing in the US under an assumed name. Ted also mentioned that Michael Riconoscuito had developed a special suitcase bomb device that could achieve near-atomic explosive yields. The CIA had a copy of the suitcase bomb design from the Wackenhut Company, where Michael Riconoscuito used to work.

At home, Edward asked Miriam about a previous operation called Gladio. Miriam informed Edward that it was a clandestine operation by NATO in Europe, where the populace was the target of false flag terror programs. The intended result was a mass hysteria about the reality of a communist takeover of Europe.

The next few days, Edward went through all that he had learnt about the plot to bomb a US landmark. Edward concluded that there would be a false flag operation involving the CIA, Mafia, Mossad and the Masonic Muslims. Edward suspected that the members listed in ZAT-911 would be those Masonic Muslims who would carry out the plot.

It was the evening of Sunday 7 July 1991, Edward was having a few drinks with Steven at a local pub. After the drinks, Edward felt intoxicated and decided to take a taxi home. Edward left his car keys with the pub owner; and gave instructions for his car to be driven back to his house the next day.

Edward woke up late with a hangover. Edward peered out of his house, but his car had not been delivered to his home. Edward then took a taxi to his office. In the afternoon, Edward received a phone call from the pub owner who informed him that his car exploded upon ignition. The driver was killed instantly. Edward knew that there was an attempt on his life.

Edward informed Casolaro about a Gladio type operation to be implemented by Masonic Muslims in the US, with the cooperation of the CIA, Mossad and the Mafia. Casolaro opined that what Edward said confirmed the operations of 'the Octopus.'

At home, Edward told Miriam about the car bomb attempt on his life. Miriam was worried. Edward had a long discussion with Miriam till way pass midnight. Suddenly, Edward heard someone's thoughts in his mind. This person was thinking of moving to the backyard of Edward's home, to block off any escape by Edward and his family. Edward told Miriam to wake up their son, Tom, and move to the back of the house. Edward went for his revolver and semi-automatic rifle. Edward met Miriam and Tom in the kitchen, at the back of the house. Edward handed his revolver to Tom. Just then, there were sounds of machine gun fire at the front of the house. Some windows at the front of the house were broken, as intruders threw bombs into the living room. The blasts from the explosions shook the whole house. Edward peered out into the backyard from the kitchen window; and saw a dark figure. Edward took a shot at the intruder who collapsed in the backyard.

There were distant wails of siren, as the living room caught fire. Edward and his family climbed over the low fence of the backyard. They ended up in the back lane. As they raced towards the front of the house, Edward saw two men with machine guns running towards a waiting car. Edward took aim with his rifle and shot one of the men. The other person managed to escape into the car which sped off. The man who was fatally shot, appeared to be Middle Eastern. Edward suspected that the ZAT-911 group was out to stop him.

Edward suddenly heard the sound of helicopter overhead. Then a helicopter landed in the middle of the road. Edward could see Jim at the door of the helicopter. Jim motioned to Edward. Edward turned around and requested Tom to take care of his mother. Edward raced towards the helicopter and boarded it.

Helicopter Night Operation

On board the helicopter, Jim briefed Edward that he had information that Edward and his family would be attacked in the night. Jim managed to gather some of his colleagues to come to the rescue of Edward and his family. Edward could see that there were three other men with Jim. These men had on body armors and all were equipped with heavy machine guns.

Edward had a hunch that the remaining attackers would be heading to Freeport, New York. Jim instructed the pilot to take them to Freeport. As they approached Freeport, they could see the cruise ship, 'Golden Horseshoe,' waiting at the landing dock. Jim directed the pilot to land the helicopter behind a warehouse. Edward together with Jim and the three men ran cautiously toward the ship. As they moved closer to the ship, they could see two cars approaching. Out of the cars jumped Middle Eastern men who raced towards the ship. One of them spotted Jim and his men; and fired his automatic rifle at them.

A firefight ensued. Jim and Edward managed to board the ship and entered into the cabin. The intense gunfight continued for another ten minutes. Suddenly, one Middle Eastern man ran out of the cabin with a suitcase. The Middle Eastern man abandoned ship, with Jim and Edward in pursuit. Edward fired his rifle and wounded the Middle Eastern man. Jim called in the helicopter which fired two missiles at the ship. There was a loud explosion and the ship was in flames.

Next morning, Jim reported to Edward that the suitcase contained a special bomb device. Steven searched the CIA database with NSA's copy of the Promis software. The database was smaller, as many Middle Eastern names were erased. Edward wondered if there would be more Gladio type operations.

Jim and Edward left the office, for a drink of water at the cooler. When they returned to the office, they found another person standing at Steven's desk. This man was making a phone call; with his back turned to Edward and Jim. As Edward and Jim entered the office, they heard the man said, ". . . kill the messenger." Then, the man put down the phone and turned around. He saw Edward and Jim; and pointed a gun at them. Jim reacted in a flash and shot the man. In a corner of the room, Edward saw Steven lying in a pool of blood.

Jim said to Edward, "We must go now!" The next few days, Jim moved Edward and his family to a number of safe houses. Finally, Jim prepared passports for Edward, Miriam and Tom under assumed names. Jim boarded Edward and his family on a Hercules transport plane, at a private airfield. In just a few hours, Edward and his family took up residence in an undisclosed location in South America.

On Saturday 10 August 1991, Casolaro was found dead in the bathtub of a motel room. His wrists were slashed open a dozen times. Local police officers were quick to conclude suicide. His briefcase containing sheaf's of documents relating to his story were missing. Without notifying his family, Casolaro's body was illegally embalmed, impeding subsequent autopsy.